Valley

OF THE

Broken Cherry Trees

Valley
of the
Broken Cherry
Trees

Lensey Namioka

Blue Heron Publishing, Inc. • Hillsboro, Oregon

Valley of the Broken Cherry Trees
By Lensey Namioka

Published by
Blue Heron Publishing, Inc.
24450 Northwest Hansen Road
Hillsboro, Oregon 97124

This paperback edition published by arrangement with the
author. Originally published in cloth by Delacorte Press.

First printing, January 1996
Manufactured in the United States of America

PUBLISHER'S CATALOGING-IN-PUBLICATION DATA

Namioka, Lensey.
Valley of the broken cherry trees.

SUMMARY: In feudal Japan two young ronin
(unemployed samurai) try to learn the identity of
the person who is mutilating the cherry trees in the
valley governed by the warlord Lord Ohmori.
[1. Samurai—Fiction. 2. Japan—History—1185–1868
—Fiction] I. Title.
PZ7.N1426Val
ISBN 0-936085-32-0

To my father-in-law
who inspired my interest in feudal Japan.

List of Characters for
VALLEY OF THE BROKEN CHERRY TREES

Zenta — a young ronin (unemployed samurai)
Matsuzo — Zenta's traveling companion
Lord Ohmori — warlord in control of the cherry tree valley
Ujinobu — Lord Ohmori's son
Lady Ayame — Lord Ohmori's daughter
Lord Kawai — the feudal overlord of the Ohmori family
Lady Sayo — wife of Lord Kawai
Torazo — Lord Kawai's fourteen-year-old son
Haru — young daughter of the local innkeeper
Wife of the innkeeper — Haru's stepmother
Gonzaemon — cousin of the innkeeper's wife
Bunkei — painter
The abbot of Sairyuji Temple
A Noh actor

刀

1

Although they had heard about the fame of the valley, the two travelers were still dazzled by their first sight of the cherry trees. The boughs were so heavily covered with blossoms that individual trees could not be distinguished. Seen close, the cherry blossoms were faintly pink near the base, but from a distance they looked white, so that the whole valley seemed veiled by a mist.

Moved by a single impulse, the two men stopped. The beauty of the cherry trees made them almost light-headed. After a moment Matsuzo, the younger of the two, sat down on a flat rock, his legs feeling suddenly weak. The two men had been climbing since early morning, but it was not fatigue that caused Matsuzo's weakness. It was the unaccustomed warmth of the spring air. They had recently traveled down from the harsh north, and his body was still not completely used to the mild temperature. He felt like closing his eyes and floating down into the valley where the soft blossoms would receive him as gently as a silk-wadded mattress.

Zenta, his companion, took off his wide, basket-shaped hat as if to feel the mild breeze against his cheeks. He sighed with pleasure and murmured, "I'm glad we came."

Matsuzo opened his eyes and glanced quickly at Zenta. It was the first time in many weeks that his companion had expressed pleasure in anything. Throughout that long, hard winter, Matsuzo had worried about his friend. Zenta had been brooding over the tragic death of his teacher, a man he regarded as a second father. More than once he had expressed disgust over their way of life, which he said was filled with senseless violence. Out of respect for his friend's grief Matsuzo had refrained from pointing out that as ronin, or unemployed samurai, they were trained only for warfare.

During that turbulent period in the last quarter of the sixteenth century, there was no shortage of opportunities for violence. Japan had been torn apart by civil wars for more than a hundred years, and the central government could not even make a pretense of controlling the country. The emperor had long ago become a shadowy figure, and Matsuzo, like most of his countrymen, had all but forgotten his existence. The military ruler, or *shogun*, was equally powerless. When Matsuzo and Zenta were in the capital a few months earlier, they saw with their own eyes that the shogun could not control even the capital city, much less the country at large.

In the provinces, rival warlords fought ceaselessly to enlarge their territories. Treachery was common, and more than one vassal warlord rose to depose his overlord. When a feudal lord was deposed, his samurai became ronin. Some of the ronin became bandits, some were fortunate enough to find new masters, and others, either through choice or necessity, wandered around taking temporary jobs. Matsuzo knew that Zenta had been a ronin since the age of fifteen, but in his ten years of wandering he had never served any one master for long.

Matsuzo himself came from an old samurai family who had lost their position after the fall of their feudal lord. Hearing of Zenta's reputation as a swordsman, formidable in one so young, Matsuzo had approached the ronin and asked to be taken on as a pupil. That had been a year ago. Since then, Matsuzo had discovered that traveling as wandering ronin with Zenta could be harrowing. Zenta had a contempt for rank and authority bordering on the reckless. Even when he was near starvation, he would refuse an offer of employment if it displeased him.

Nevertheless, Matsuzo continued to follow Zenta, for he soon learned that beneath his severity Zenta had a deep compassion for people in trouble. This appealed to Matsuzo's own generous nature. He also learned that Zenta's reserve was not coldness but the result of an early tragedy, which left him wary of emotional entanglements.

The past few months had been harsh. Depressed by his teacher's death, Zenta was sunk in gloom and hardly bothered even to look for shelter. It was Matsuzo who took the initiative in seeking employment for the two of them. He had not been very successful in finding lucrative work, however. For a while some farmers gave them food and shelter in return for keeping away bandits who had been harassing the region. But the farmers were poor and could barely feed themselves, let alone two extra mouths.

After the lean winter, Matsuzo now felt as hungry as a wild animal just awakened from its long winter sleep. He glanced at his companion. Even when Zenta was in the best of condition, his build was spare, and now his eyes were sunken and the hollowness of his cheeks was accentuated by a stubble of beard. Matsuzo realized that he himself looked not much better. Normally his appearance was pleasant enough — the interested glances of the girls he passed in his travels gave proof of that. But now, with unkempt hair and dusty clothes, Matsuzo knew that he and Zenta made a hungry and dangerous-looking pair. Small wonder that the people they met on the road kept their distance.

Zenta put back his hat and smiled at Matsuzo with some of his old spirit. "Let's go down to the inn. I'm famished."

As the two men descended into the valley, Matsuzo said, "Are you sure the innkeeper still remembers you? I don't know what we'll do if he doesn't invite us to stay. We haven't any money left at all."

"He can't have forgotten," said Zenta. "It's only been two years since I saved his family from some soldiers. There was a battle nearby and the soldiers were looting all the houses in the area. When I arrived they were on the point of attacking the innkeeper's wife and daughter."

Matsuzo had to agree that the innkeeper was unlikely to forget the incident. Coming to the valley to look at its famous cherry trees had been his idea, and when Zenta mentioned that an innkeeper in the area could be counted on to offer hospitality, Matsuzo had been overjoyed.

"We can certainly use a good meal," said Zenta. It was his way of apologizing for his failure to provide for the two of them that winter.

Matsuzo's spirits rose. Zenta seemed, finally, to be coming out of his gloom. Eagerly anticipating the meal soon to be set in front of them, the two ronin quickened their steps. Zenta had described the inn as luxurious, and the cooking was certain to be outstanding.

Matsuzo's pleasant thoughts were interrupted by shouting. He looked around and discovered that Zenta had fallen behind and was staring back at a farmhouse which they had just passed.

In front of the house was a man thrashing a boy with a stick. "You thief! You thought I wouldn't catch you, didn't you?"

"Probably a starving boy who stole a radish," said Matsuzo pityingly. Because of his own hunger, he felt for anyone who was driven to stealing food.

Zenta was frowning. "There is something strange here. I'm not sure I like the looks of this."

Matsuzo looked again and saw that something was indeed unusual. All the shouting came from the man delivering the blows. The boy, who was dwarfed by the big, husky farmer, was nevertheless trying to grab the stick away from his tormentor. The blows that landed on his arms and shoulders must have been extremely painful, but he didn't utter a sound. There was something unnerving about his obstinate silence. "I'd better find out what this is about," said Zenta, and started for the farmhouse. He reached the farmer just as the latter aimed a vicious blow that could have maimed the boy if it had landed. Zenta seized the farmer's wrist and wrenched the stick away.

The farmer turned furiously and started to launch himself toward Zenta, but he was brought up short by the sight of the ronin's two swords. "What business is it of yours to interfere?" he snarled. "He's just getting what he deserves!"

Matsuzo approached the boy, who was straightening his clothes. "Did he hurt you badly?" the young ronin asked.

The boy did not answer. On his face appeared such a malevolent expression that Matsuzo involuntarily retreated a step. He had seldom seen an uglier face. Under a low forehead the boy had thick, black eyebrows that nearly met over his nose. The nose was broad, and his lips, which were bleeding, looked coarse. The boy must have bitten down hard on them to prevent himself from crying out. His face was not his most unattractive feature, however. His long arms and big hands, all out of proportion to his short stature, looked clumsy and ungainly as he fumbled to tie his sash.

Meanwhile Zenta was questioning the farmer. "What has the boy done? Surely he didn't deserve a beating like that?"

4

"He stole my pheasant, the one I trapped only this morning," said the farmer. "I was going to sell it to the innkeeper for a good sum of money."

Zenta looked around. "The pheasant must still be on the ground somewhere. Why don't we look for it? You can still sell it, can't you?"

"I did look!" shouted the farmer. "There is no trace of the bird. I asked the boy where he put it, but he only jeered at me and laughed."

"How do you know that he stole the pheasant in the first place?" asked Zenta.

At the question the farmer nearly gibbered with rage. "Of course he stole it! He's always sneaking around the neighborhood. I'm sure he steals from other people, too."

"That's a lie!" This came from the boy, and Matsuzo looked at him in astonishment. The boy's voice had cracked in the middle, and Matsuzo realized that he was younger than he had at first appeared. His face had a curious maturity, but his voice gave away his true age, which was around thirteen or fourteen. "I didn't steal your pheasant," continued the boy. "It was stolen by your neighbor's daughter, the one who is always making eyes at you."

Matsuzo was shocked by what looked like a leer on the boy's coarse and bloody lips. The farmer's face turned dark red, and he made another rush at the boy. "Why, you dirty little sneak!"

Zenta reached out almost lazily and held the farmer back, immobilizing him with an arm lock. "Just a moment. Do you have any proof that he was the thief?"

The farmer writhed in Zenta's hands. "No, but — "

"In that case you don't need me anymore," said the boy. He smiled sardonically at the three men, but his eyes were cold and implacable. He turned and walked away, holding himself with dignity, although the stiff set of his shoulders betrayed his pain.

When the boy turned a corner and went out of sight, Zenta released the farmer. "Don't bother chasing him. You might find yourself in more trouble than it's worth."

Leaving the farmer hopping with frustration, the two men continued on their way. "Maybe he should question the neighbor's daughter," remarked Matsuzo.

"I think so, too," said Zenta. "That boy was telling the truth. What did you make of him?"

"Well, he comes from a good family," said Matsuzo. "That is obvious from his voice and his speech. He didn't want us to know, and that's why he tried to keep silent."

Zenta nodded. "Samurai family, of course. But his behavior was odd — and disturbing too. I'd hate to face him on a battlefield when he grows up."

"*If* he grows up," said Matsuzo. "He seems to have a gift for making enemies."

"It's a pity about the pheasant though," said Zenta dreamily. "I like pheasant stewed with ginkgo nuts."

At the mention of food Matsuzo's mouth filled and he had to swallow. "They are bound to serve delicious freshwater fish down at the inn. Look at this mountain stream. I can almost see the fish jumping."

The little stream which they were following dropped abruptly over some rocks, and at the bottom of the waterfall was a clearing with half a dozen cherry trees. The arrangement of the trees was so picturesque that they could only have been planted deliberately, unlike the wild cherry trees they had seen so far. Beyond the haze of the cherry blossoms they could see a bamboo fence enclosing a large house with a thatched roof.

Matsuzo looked questioningly at his companion. "Is that…"

"Yes, that's the inn," said Zenta.

Their path had become steep, and it finally changed into a flight of steps slippery with moss. With Zenta leading the way, the two men descended carefully and found themselves in the clearing under the cherry trees. It was like having a canopy overhead. More than any other flower the cherry blossom symbolized nature at its most beautiful. The two ronin stood still, captured by the enchantment of the blossoms, and for a moment a feeling almost of religious awe passed over them. Then Zenta stirred. "Let's go down to the inn."

But Matsuzo hung back, staring at a tree which had a curiously lopsided look. "What a hideous job of pruning!" he said, shocked. He could see from the stump that a sizable limb had been removed, permanently spoiling the shape of the old and valuable tree. No gardener as incompetent as this should have been allowed to touch the tree!

Zenta was not looking at the crippled tree, however, but at the entrance to the inn. "Look, there are two samurai standing guard, and they are wearing the Ohmori crest on their kimonos!"

Lord Ohmori was a feudal lord whose domain included the whole of the valley. Why should his samurai be guarding a public inn? There could be a number of explanations, not all of them pleasant.

Matsuzo turned to Zenta. "I hope this doesn't mean the innkeeper has done something to offend Lord Ohmori and is under arrest." His hopes of a delicious meal and a hot bath began to fade.

Zenta shook his head. "I don't think the innkeeper has been arrested. They would have dragged him off to prison, not posted guards around the inn like this."

Before Matsuzo could stop him, Zenta was moving toward the front entrance of the inn. At his approach, the guards stiffened to attention. "State your names and your business here!" snapped one of the guards.

"My name is Konishi Zenta," replied Zenta, "and I'm an acquaintance of the family here."

"The inn is occupied," said the guard. "You can't come in unless you have business here."

They heard a sound of light footsteps, and a girl appeared behind them carrying a basket of wild mountain vegetables. She was about fifteen years old, very pretty in her homespun kimono. Over her kimono she wore a patterned apron, and around her head was a white kerchief which set off her soft, round cheeks.

At the sight of the girl, Zenta called, "Haru! Do you still remember me?"

The girl called Haru stopped and stared at the two ronin. Suddenly she dropped her basket and ran over to Zenta. "You've come back!" she cried, and bowed down before him until her head nearly touched the ground. When she rose there were tears in her eyes. "You left so quickly that we had no chance to thank you. My father will be overjoyed to see you!"

"Then you know these men?" asked the guard.

"This gentleman saved our lives," said Haru. "You must let them come in."

The guard lowered his spear. "Very well, if you and your father will vouch for them."

As they passed through the front gate Zenta asked, "Why are

7

these Ohmori samurai guarding your house?"

Haru lowered her voice. "Lord Ohmori and his family are staying with us in order to view the cherry blossoms here. It is a great honor for us, of course, but it does keep us quite busy."

A great honor indeed, thought Matsuzo. He had known that this was a luxury inn, but hadn't thought it was grand enough to accommodate a feudal lord. Perhaps the cherry blossoms here were exceptional.

They were crossing the front courtyard, which was immaculately groomed. The stepping stones were carefully set in a bed of thick green moss, and beyond the moss was white sand swept to make wavelike swirls. Here and there were islands of rock and shrubbery, sculptured into smooth mounds. Matsuzo could see that the courtyard was tended by an accomplished gardener obviously not the one who had butchered the cherry tree outside.

Beyond the courtyard was the main guest house of the inn. A substantial building consisting of two parts set at right angles to each other, the house was more like the private mansion of a wealthy man than a public post station for travelers. The light brown thatched roof with its neatly trimmed edges looked fresh and clean. What they could see of the sliding wall panels had paper of a dazzling white, and through one of the open panels gleamed the wooden floor of the corridor, polished to a mirrorlike smoothness.

Haru led the two ronin past the main guest house to a smaller building. "This is where our family and the staff live," she said, and stepped up to the entrance hall.

As the two men removed their sandals and followed her up to the house, Haru, said, "Please wait here. I'll go and look for my father."

Matsuzo was fascinated by a tiny dimple which appeared and disappeared in Haru's cheek as she talked. "A very attractive girl," he said when Haru had left. "I have a feeling that our visit here is going to be a pleasant one."

Zenta grinned. "I'm afraid Haru will be quite busy with her important guests."

Matsuzo's face fell. "They do look busy here. Perhaps that guard was right. The inn may be fully occupied."

Before Zenta could reply, the inside door opened and Haru appeared with her father. The innkeeper, a small, balding man, was nearly weeping with emotion. Like his daughter he bowed down to the ground. "At last, at last!" he cried. "Now I can thank you properly for your noble action two years ago!"

Zenta looked acutely embarrassed by the innkeeper's effusive greeting. He mumbled something unintelligible and seemed almost sorry that he had come.

"You can ask me for anything — anything at all!" declared the innkeeper, finally scrambling to his feet.

"Well, could we have some supper, then?" asked Zenta.

"I'll order the kitchen to get busy right away!" said the innkeeper.

"And, Father, we should prepare a room for them to stay," added Haru.

"I'll see to it immediately," said her father.

"Just a moment," said a new voice. A tall, slim woman came into the room and closed the door behind her. Everything about her was smooth and polished. Her face was a pale, perfect oval, and it was framed by hair that had the deep sheen of really expensive lacquer. She looked at the innkeeper, and when he refused to meet her eye, she turned to the girl. "Haru, who are these two men?"

Haru's lips tightened. "This gentleman was the samurai who saved my mother and me from the soldiers." She glanced at her father for support, but he said nothing. "You have heard us talking about it often enough!" she told the woman. "If it weren't for him, our inn would have been looted and set on fire!"

The woman ignored Haru's tone. Turning to the innkeeper she said, "So...you are prepared to show your gratitude. What are you intending to do?"

"They are not asking for much," replied the innkeeper hurriedly. "They just want some food and a place to stay."

The woman smiled coldly. "They can't stay here. We're completely full."

"Isn't that for the mistress here to decide?" suggested Zenta. His tone was polite and Matsuzo marveled at his self-control. He himself was seething.

At Zenta's words the woman laughed aloud. "*I* am the mistress!"

"My wife — the one you saved — died last year," explained the innkeeper wretchedly to Zenta. "This is my present wife."

"Why not give these people some money, and they can find lodging elsewhere," suggested the woman. As she turned to leave, she said to Haru, "You've wasted enough time here. Hurry and attend to our guests. They're impatient for their dinner."

When the door closed after her, the innkeeper looked helplessly at the two ronin. "Please," he begged, "she has been working too hard because of our important guests. She is not her usual self."

"On the contrary, she is exactly her usual self," muttered Haru.

"Really, Haru..." protested the innkeeper feebly. Zenta rose. "We must not keep you from your important guests."

"Wait! I have an idea!" said Haru. "These two gentlemen can stay with Bunkei, the artist."

"That's an excellent idea, Haru!" cried the innkeeper, beaming with relief. "Bunkei's house has plenty of room."

"They can wash in our bathroom here," added Haru. "The water has been heated already."

"And we can send over some food from our kitchen," said the innkeeper.

"We have been doing that already," said Haru. But her father was bustling out to give orders and did not hear her remark.

"Who is this artist?" asked Zenta. "Won't he mind if two uninvited guests descend on him?"

"Bunkei is a painter," replied Haru. "Since he doesn't have much money, we let him live in a tea house which belongs to our family. It's very close."

"Some artists don't like to be disturbed when they're working," said Matsuzo. He wrote poetry himself and he often said that concentration was essential for creative work.

"Don't worry, Bunkei loves company," said Haru cheerfully. "Besides, he has a guest already."

Matsuzo thought he detected a note of malice in Haru's voice. But he was so glad to have found shelter that he refused to worry about who the other guest was.

2

After his bath Matsuzo was still as hungry as a wild animal but he was glad he no longer looked like one. He put on the clean kimono Haru had brought and decided that the girl had taste in addition to her good looks.

"Let's go," said Zenta impatiently, as Matsuzo finished tying his sash.

The house of the artist Bunkei was outside the fence encircling the inn and its gardens. According to Haru, before their house became an inn it had originally belonged to a wealthy samurai who had chosen the site for its view of the cherry trees. He had the tea house built a little distance away from the main house so that he could practice the cult of tea ceremony without distraction.

With a serving girl leading the way, the two ronin found the house at the end of a tiny bamboo grove behind the inn. It was a small house, with yellow clay walls and a thatched roof on which a few weeds were growing. The effect, probably intentional, was charmingly rustic. A magnificent cherry tree framed the entranceway.

At the sight of the tree the two men stopped dead. "That same gardener must have pruned this tree, too!" exclaimed Matsuzo, horrified.

The tree was planted next to the house, and one of its lateral branches had been trained to hang over the entrance. Or it would have if the limb had not been chopped off abruptly. It was outrageous

11

that a gardener as incompetent as this one should have been allowed to work here.

"Maybe there is some disease affecting the cherry trees in this area," said Zenta, "and the sick branch had to be chopped off quickly to prevent the disease from spreading to the rest of the tree."

There was no time to speculate further on the cherry tree. The serving girl slid open the door of Bunkei's house and announced their arrival. The artist was evidently expecting them, for he appeared immediately. "Please enter. You have come at just the right time. The dinner is already set out."

The serving girl having bowed and left, the two ronin entered the main room of the small house. Matsuzo examined the artist curiously. From Haru's description he had expected to find a plump, lively man with a cheerful smile. Bunkei was indeed plump, but his face, with sagging cheeks and dark bags under the eyes, looked more gloomy than cheerful. The brown kimono he wore was wrinkled and had patches down the front that looked like wine stains adding to his air of carelessness and dejection.

Bunkei's welcome to the two ronin was friendly enough. He invited Zenta to take the flat cushion placed at the seat of honor, and after a decent show of reluctance Zenta sat down. Matsuzo was placed at Zenta's right, across from the artist. Each person had two lacquered trays in front of him, with food prepared to delight the eye as well as the palate.

Bunkei took upon himself the duties of a host. "We have to serve ourselves, since the maids are needed back at the inn," he apologized. He sighed. "I don't have much appetite these days, and this plain food does little to tempt me. I hope you gentlemen will overlook our deficiencies."

The two ronin needed little urging to eat, and for a time conversation lagged as they applied themselves to the dinner. Matsuzo uncovered the lid of the soup bowl and took a sip of the soup, which was clear and flavored faintly with tiny mushrooms. After eating a mouthful of rice, he attacked the grilled freshwater fish. It was so savory that he found it hard not to cram the whole piece into his mouth. In a deep dish he found burdock root boiled with chestnuts, which melted on his tongue. A small plate contained fish cake, dyed red on the outside and sliced to resemble cherry blossoms. Beside it was a dish of fern tips, which Matsuzo had seen earlier in Haru's basket, now blanched and covered with a sesame sauce. It was all Matsuzo could do not to make a spectacle of himself by gobbling down his food.

Across from Matsuzo, Zenta was eating with the efficiency and dispatch of a man who did not know where he would get his next meal. Bunkei, in spite of his professed lack of appetite, ate almost as heartily as the two guests.

By the time Matsuzo had finished his third bowl of rice his hunger was less desperate and he was able to pause in his eating and look around the room. It was a very comfortable room, with the floor covered completely by eight tatami mats. The side of the room facing Matsuzo had sliding panels leading to the outside. One panel was left open, and he could see the bamboo grove, a soft green in the evening light. Now and then a breeze brought a drift of cherry petals, like falling snow.

In the alcove behind Zenta was a dramatic black-and-white ink painting. It displayed a thick brush stroke slashing down diagonally and ending in a series of small squiggles. Try as he might, Matsuzo could not determine what the subject of the painting was. He peered at the line of writing in one corner of the painting, but it proved to be as mystifying as the picture. It hinted that the forces of spring could not be restrained. Matsuzo stared at the painting again, but was no more successful the second time in finding anything recognizable.

"Ah, I see that you are looking at my work," said Bunkei. He gave a delicate belch. "Thoughts that are too deep for words have to be expressed by the brush."

"Of course," said Matsuzo hurriedly. Both the picture and the words were too deep for him. He merely nodded, gravely.

The artist picked up a piece of fish with his chopsticks and waved it at the painting. "Shallow-minded people, like those silly maids from the inn, dare to call that stroke a squiggle!"

Zenta, who had been eating with single-minded concentration, glanced up in surprise at Bunkei's vehemence, and turned around to look at the painting.

Bunkei frowned, brooding over the insult. "A squiggle!"

Zenta choked and began to cough. Matsuzo looked suspiciously at his friend's crimson face. He didn't see anything remotely funny about Bunkei's suffering at the hands of ignorant, insensitive critics.

Then why did Zenta look as if he were laughing? "What's the matter with you?" Matsuzo asked.

"Just a...fish bone...stuck in my throat," sputtered Zenta.

"A mouthful of rice will push the fish bone down," suggested the artist.

"I'm all right now," gasped Zenta. He took a deep breath and steadied himself.

For the first time Bunkei looked carefully at Zenta. "Haru told me just now that you were the man who saved her and her mother from a score of enemy soldiers. Everyone in this valley knows about the incident."

Zenta shifted uncomfortably on his cushion. "Those soldiers were drunk," he muttered.

"The innkeeper and his wife talked about it often — his first wife, I should say. She was a woman who understood proper gratitude."

"Haru must take after her mother," said Matsuzo. "Haru is a good girl — except, of course, for her insensitivity to art," said Bunkei. "But her mother, now, there was a really fine woman. I painted a masterpiece on one of their folding screens. She was so grateful that she let me stay permanently in this house. The inn and the tea house used to belong to her family, you know."

"The new wife is different," said Matsuzo, remembering the woman's insolent eyes and her small, mean mouth.

At the mention of the innkeeper's new wife Bunkei's eyes flashed angrily. "That woman wanted to drive me from this house! She said her cousin had arrived and needed a place to stay."

"Doesn't the innkeeper have any say at all?" asked Matsuzo.

"He does anything she wants," said Bunkei disgustedly. "Fortunately he respected the wishes of his dead wife in this case and insisted that I remain. But I have to share this crowded house with that woman's cousin."

Matsuzo flushed. "It's even more crowded now that you have to share it with us, too."

"Oh, I'm delighted to have *you*," said Bunkei hurriedly. "I just can't stand the cousin — silly fellow, always tiptoeing around looking mysterious. He must be a spy."

Zenta looked up from his rice bowl. "A spy? Who is paying him?"

"I don't know," said Bunkei indifferently. "Maybe he has connec-

14

tions with the Ohmori family. He visits the main house of the inn often enough." The artist paused and his face became thoughtful. "I've heard that Lord Ohmori is a man of discerning taste. I wonder if he is interested in buying paintings?"

Zenta had finished his fish and was starting on the pickles. "It's strange that the Ohmori family should be staying here at the inn and not at Sairyuji Temple. The abbot there is descended from a noble family, and the temple would have more fitting accommodations for people of rank than an inn."

"Perhaps Lord Ohmori wants to stay at the inn because the cherry trees are more beautiful over here," suggested Matsuzo.

Zenta shook his head. "The cherry trees near Sairyuji Temple are just as beautiful as the ones here."

"I think I know the reason why Lord Ohmori is not staying at the temple," said Bunkei. "There is talk that someone else is staying there already."

"I wonder who it could be!" said Zenta. "Lord Ohmori controls this whole region, and no one here outranks him. Why does he have to yield the guest rooms at the temple and put up at an inn?"

For a while the three men ate in silence. Zenta finally put his chopsticks back on the holder, replaced the lid on the soup bowl, and sat back with a sigh of content. "By the way," he said, "does Lord Ohmori or one of his samurai have a son, a boy about thirteen or fourteen years old?"

Bunkei shook his head. "As far as I know, Lord Ohmori has only one son, and he is in his twenties."

"The boy we saw was very ugly," said Matsuzo. "He looked as if he had a grudge against everybody."

Bunkei's face cleared. "Ah, I know the boy you mean. I've seen him about, usually in the evenings. He seems to hang around Haru a great deal."

Matsuzo was shocked. "But he's only a boy! His voice is still changing!"

Bunkei laughed. "It isn't what you think. Haru only feels sorry for him because he always looks forlorn and friendless."

He broke off and stared as Zenta got up noiselessly and walked over to the sliding door. With a swift jerk the ronin swept open the door. Standing outside in the corridor was a man looking at them

15

with an innocent expression.

The newcomer bowed politely and entered the room. "I am Sasaki Gonzaemon. The innkeeper's wife is my cousin."

So this was their mysterious fellow guest, thought Matsuzo. Gonzaemon was somewhat above medium height and muscular in build, and he wore the two swords of a samurai. He removed the longer one and placed it on the floor. Then he reached behind him to bring out a large earthenware jug of sake. "My cousin thought the wine would go well with your dinner."

Bunkei had turned surly when Gonzaemon entered the room, but at the sight of the jug he unbent slightly. "Well, it's a bit late for sake, since we've almost finished eating," he grumbled, getting to his feet. "I'll go and get the wine heated."

"We don't have to bother," said Gonzaemon. "This is the best grade of sake at the inn, and it doesn't need heating to bring out the flavor."

Matsuzo began to understand some of Bunkei's irritation with the man, for Gonzaemon radiated an air of self-satisfaction. Even more annoying was his smile: it was a dazzling smile, full of big white teeth.

In addition to the sake, Gonzaemon had also brought small dishes of food to accompany the wine. The sake was as good as he had claimed, and when he served it he assumed the manners of a gracious host. With Gonzaemon's arrival, Bunkei had somehow been relegated to the position of an uninvited guest.

The artist was not to be pushed into the background without a struggle, however. He began with disparaging remarks about the dishes of food Gonzaemon was setting out. "This fish is poor stuff," he sneered. "The best thing to go with this particular wine is raw squid."

Gonzaemon merely turned on his dazzling smile again. "I'm a mountain man, myself, and I have never been to the sea. Therefore I have never tasted raw squid. But this fish is passable; it's what the guests at the inn are eating."

The artist continued to grumble, but by the time he finished his fifth cup of sake, his resentment had become less vocal. He turned his back on Gonzaemon and began to address all his remarks to Matsuzo.

Mellowed by the excellent sake, the young ronin felt a strong urge to lie down on the springy tatami mat and close his eyes. He realized, however, that the artist was condescending to explain the painting to him. It was a great honor, and he struggled to stay alert.

"Observe that brush stroke," hiccuped Bunkei. "To an untrained eye it looks like a stroke any child could make. But I had to train for forty years before I could do it. Those ignorant maids from the inn said it took me only three seconds to paint that picture. It actually took me forty years!"

Surprise jerked Matsuzo awake from his pleasant reverie of cherry blossoms and pretty girls with dimples. He was surprised to find himself lying on his back, and he tried to sit up. Did Bunkei really say forty years? Looking at the artist, Matsuzo estimated that Bunkei had started to paint before he could walk.

The artist was now inclined to be tearful. "Every day of those forty years was filled with suffering. You don't know the pain of being a sensitive artist surrounded by crassness and stupidity.

Matsuzo finally decided that Bunkei did not always speak the literal truth. But one had to allow artists a certain latitude, for they could not be bound by the same rules as other people. Now that he was sitting up, Matsuzo noticed Zenta and Gonzaemon convening at the other side of the room.

"And what did you do before you came to this valley?" Gonzaemon was asking. He raised the sake jug to pour.

Zenta indicated that his cup was still full. He seldom drank to excess — wine interfered with his concentration, he often said. To Gonzaemon's question he replied, "Oh, we did this and that. We didn't have much choice."

Gonzaemon persisted. "But surely, with your reputation you could have had any number of offers? People here had heard of you even before the affair of the soldiers two years ago."

Zenta was looking increasingly bored. "I couldn't always accept the offers," he said shortly.

Gonzaemon's inquisitiveness only sharpened. "Because of ill health, you mean? But you are recovered now?"

Matsuzo thought Gonzaemon's questions impertinent, and he expected Zenta to make the kind of cutting rejoinder he usually did when questioned about his personal life.

Instead, Zenta said, "You seem to know a great deal about local affairs. Can you tell me anything about a young boy, thirteen or fourteen years old, who seems to be of samurai family?"

Gonzaemon barely hesitated in his answer. "No, I don't know anything about him."

Bunkei, who gave every appearance of being fast asleep, suddenly sat up. "I saw you talking to him. You were just down by the waterfall, in fact."

For a moment Gonzaemon paused. Then he flashed his white teeth in a smile. "Oh, that boy! I did bump into him one evening as he was running away from the inn, and I asked him what he was doing. He seemed to be in a hurry."

Zenta was no longer looking bored. "Did the boy say anything to you?"

"No, he simply rushed off," replied Gonzaemon. He seemed anxious to change the subject.

"That's a lie," said Bunkei, emptying his cup. "The boy was saying something about coming here again the following night."

Matsuzo guessed that Bunkei was deliberately provoking Gonzaemon because of the latter's contemptuous treatment of him. The bland good humor disappeared momentarily from Gonzaemon's face, but then he smiled again and said, "You couldn't have heard right. You are drunk most evenings."

"You supply me with wine when it suits you, but that doesn't mean I drink it all immediately," retorted Bunkei. He reached for the sake jug, shook it, and poured the rest into his cup. After emptying his cup he lay down on the tatami mat. "Don't bother to wake me if the boy comes again tonight."

Gonzaemon stood up and looked down at the sleeping form of the artist. His lips were set, and such an ugly look came into his face that for a moment Matsuzo was alarmed for Bunkei's safety. Why was the artist's remark about the mysterious boy so provocative? Then Gonzaemon relaxed and gave an indifferent shrug. "I'll show you to your room," he said to the two ronin. "We can talk there without being constantly interrupted by this fat fool."

The two ronin followed Gonzaemon into a clean, airy room where mattresses had already been spread out by the maids. The room was not large, the floor area being only the size of four and a half tatami mats but there was room for Zenta and Gonzaemon to seat themselves on the mats with their backs against a wall.

Matsuzo felt nothing but an overwhelming desire for bed, and he stretched out on one of the mattresses. For a moment his attention was caught when he heard Zenta asking Gonzaemon about the identity of the visitors at Sairyuji Temple. After he heard Gonzaemon reply that he knew nothing about them, Matsuzo let himself drift away. He fell asleep listening to the low conversation between the other two men as they discussed various schools of swordsmanship and master swordsmen they had met.

3
三

From the next room came the soft rumble of Bunkei's snores. Zenta glanced across at Matsuzo and saw that he, too, was still fast asleep. In the diffuse morning light coming through the paper screens, Matsuzo looked younger than that strangely mature boy they had seen on the previous afternoon. Quietly Zenta opened the door to the veranda and slipped outside. He smiled, thinking that Matsuzo would probably wake with a fierce headache from the sake. Perhaps he and the artist could keep each other company in their misery. As he closed the door, Zenta thought he heard a check in Bunkei's snores but they soon resumed a regular rhythm.

Stepping down from the veranda, Zenta stooped and washed his face at a stone basin which was filled with water dripping from a bamboo pipe. The water, piped directly from a mountain stream, was stinging cold. He felt sluggish, the result of eating too well the previous night, after weeks of privation. The cold water refreshed him.

He had seen no sign of their fellow guest this morning. The door to Gonzaemon's room was open, the mattress folded away and the room bare. Zenta thought over the conversation he had held with the man. Bunkei was probably right: Gonzaemon asked questions like a spy. But his curiosity was so open and his questions so direct that it was hard to take offense at them. On the other hand, Zenta was convinced that Gonzaemon was a genuine swordsman. The fencing schools he had attended and the masters he had known showed that he possessed more than the routine interest in the sword required of every samurai. As Zenta finished drying his face, he decided that Gonzaemon, in discussing schools of swordsmanship with him, was not merely satisfying an idle curiosity about Zenta's skill. Gonzaemon showed signs of wanting to recruit him.

The early morning mist was finally disappearing as the sun probed its way into the valley. Zenta walked to the small clearing under the cherry trees. The place had the hush of a Shinto shrine. The morning light tinted the blossoms pink, and again their beauty intoxicated him. Why trouble himself with Gonzaemon's behavior? He had come to this valley to enjoy cherry blossoms, and he was not interested in being recruited. He had no need for money. For the time being, the hospitality of Haru and her father supplied all his wants.

But one thing disturbed his peace of mind: the meeting with the strange boy. More than anything else Zenta admired courage. He remembered the proud way the boy had marched off, disdaining help, yet obviously in pain. For all his arrogance, the boy looked desperately unhappy. Zenta himself had been only a year or so older when he became a ronin, and he remembered his loneliness and despair at the time. It was quite possible that he might not have survived at all if he had not met the kindly old man who was to become his teacher. And now this boy was in trouble and needed support. Zenta had an urgent feeling that he had better find the boy soon, or something tragic might happen. Remembering the bitterness in the boy's eyes, he wondered if it were not already too late.

Haru might know something. Zenta recalled Bunkei's remark that he had seen the boy with Haru. At the moment the girl was likely busy serving breakfast to the guests at the inn, but if he could see her for only a moment, he might at least find out the name of the boy and where he lived. Zenta decided to visit the inn before the maids came to Bunkei's house with breakfast.

Just as he reached the gate of the inn, it opened and one of the samurai guards came out. When he saw Zenta he looked surprised. "How did you know?" he asked.

Zenta was equally surprised. "How did I know what?"

"How did you know you were sent for?" demanded the guard.

"I didn't know I was sent for," replied Zenta, wondering who had sent for him, and why.

Shaking his head in bewilderment the guard said, "All right, follow me. The young master is waiting for you."

"The young master?" asked Zenta, following the guard into the inn. "Would that be Lord Ohmori?"

"The young master is Lord Ujinobu, Lord Ohmori's son," said the guard.

They walked through the hallway of the inn, past some maids who were carrying breakfast trays back to the kitchen. Zenta hoped that he would see Haru and arrange to meet her later, but she was not in sight.

The guard finally stopped at a door, pushed it open a crack, and said, "My lord, here is the ronin you asked for."

"Have him come in," said a voice from the room. Zenta entered and bowed deeply by the door. Raising his head, he saw a young man in his early twenties seated on a large, flat silk cushion. Ohmori Ujinobu had sharp-cut features, a thin nose, and a slightly pointed chin. Zenta found it an intelligent, sensitive face, but he thought that a looseness about the mouth indicated weakness of character.

Now that Ujinobu saw the man he had sent for, he seemed at a loss about how to proceed. Finally he said, "Yes, well, the innkeeper told us about what happened here two years ago. It appears that when our troops retreated after the battle here — a planned withdrawal, of course — some enemy soldiers started looting the inn. You came and drove those soldiers away single-handedly."

Zenta suppressed a sigh. He was tired of hearing about the incident of the soldiers and wished heartily that the innkeeper had gossiped less.

Ujinobu toyed with a tassel of the cushion he was sitting on. Zenta knew men of Ujinobu's type and had little patience with them. On a few occasions he had been hired to give lessons in swordsmanship to young men like this — spoiled sons of wealthy samurai or feudal lords. They were willing enough to undergo hard training for a time, but they soon grew bored. Zenta wished that Ujinobu would come to the point, for he longed to have a talk with Haru. He was also very hungry and looked forward to joining Matsuzo and Bunkei for breakfast.

Ujinobu dropped the tassel he was combing with his fingers and asked abruptly, "Are you in service with anyone?"

"No, my lord, I'm not in anyone's service at present," answered Zenta. When Gonzaemon had asked him the same question, he had given a short answer but he couldn't treat Ujinobu quite so unceremoniously.

"Well, would you like to take a position with our family?" asked Ujinobu.

Zenta made no effort to hide his astonishment. Hiring retainers was a matter for the officer in charge of the household samurai, not something the son of the feudal lord should meddle in. "Why?" asked Zenta. He realized that he was being disrespectful, but the interview was unexpected, and he was curious to see how Ujinobu would react.

"Eh?" asked Ujinobu, looking nonplussed. Zenta's reply rendered him momentarily speechless. Then he rallied. "What do you mean, why? I'm offering you a job!"

"You have plenty of samurai here," said Zenta. "At a rough estimate, I'd say that you have more than twenty men at the inn. That's an adequate retinue for a cherry-viewing party, especially when it's deep in your own territory. Why should you have to hire an extra retainer?"

Somewhat tardily, Ujinobu began to show offense. "I would have thought that working for the Ohmori family would be a great honor," he said stiffly. Then his tone grew spiteful. "Especially for a starving ronin!"

Zenta bowed his head and waited for dismissal. After a moment of silence he noticed that Ujinobu was not looking at him at all. He was staring at a painted folding screen which partitioned off one corner of the room. From the thick, bold brush strokes, which had a tendency to end in little squiggles, Zenta guessed that the screen was Bunkei's masterpiece, the work that had earned him tenure at the tea house.

When he first entered the room, Zenta had automatically assumed that the screen was there to partition off Ujinobu's bed, but now he realized that the maids must have folded away the bed before they served breakfast. What was behind the screen? Or rather, who was behind the screen?

Ujinobu was looking anxiously at the screen, almost as if hoping for a cue. Suddenly his face cleared. "Ah, yes," he said to Zenta. "I've been told that you are making inquiries about a young boy."

Zenta was startled. Now, how could Ujinobu have heard that? The only two people he had asked were Bunkei and Gonzaemon. The artist was snoring away in a drunken sleep, and Gonzaemon had disappeared. Could the latter be a spy for the Ohmori family? But that made little sense. Why should the Ohmoris employ a spy for their own cherry-viewing party?

"I am to tell you that the boy is no concern of yours," continued Ujinobu. "It would be healthier for you if you forgot his existence." With that, he nodded his head haughtily in dismissal.

Zenta bowed deeply and withdrew. As he walked down the corridor in search of Haru, he thought over Ujinobu's words. The use of the phrase "I am to tell you" showed that Ujinobu was a spokesman for someone else — the person behind the screen, perhaps. That person wanted him to keep away from the boy.

Then there was the puzzle of why the Ohmoris wanted to hire him. Zenta was under no illusion that the Ohmoris had offered him the position because of his reputation as a swordsman. They had some specific job in mind. Whatever it was, it was not something they wanted their own men to perform. When a particularly treacherous or dishonorable act was contemplated, it was sometimes the practice to hire a ronin — an unattached samurai with no allegiances. During these turbulent times there were thousands of ronin at large, and some of them were hungry enough to set aside their scruples and the warrior's code. But Zenta hoped that he would never have to compromise his honor. That was why he was usually starving.

Why had Ujinobu been the one to approach him? If the Ohmori family wanted to hire a ronin, it would be the job of some senior officer to do so. Could it be possible that Ujinobu wanted to do something behind his father's back? Remembering Ujinobu's wantonness, Zenta thought that whatever the job was, it had to be unsavory.

Zenta finally found a maid who led him to Haru. In the garden outside the kitchen, Haru and two other girls were hanging out quilts and mattresses to air in the sun. The richly colored quilts and the girls in their homespun blue-and-white kimonos made a charming picture against a background of cherry trees.

When Zenta first saw Haru two years ago, she had been hardly more than a child, a frightened child with tears streaming down her face. Now she was taking her duties seriously as the daughter of the innkeeper. "Fluff that quilt out a little more," she directed one of the maids.

On seeing Zenta, all three girls bowed deeply, the two maids covering their mouths with their hands to hide embarrassed giggles. Haru smiled in welcome. "Good morning, sir. Have you slept well? I've already given orders for your breakfast and it will be brought to the tea house in a minute."

Zenta smiled back. "You don't have to hurry with the breakfast. I doubt if Matsuzo or Bunkei are awake yet."

"I'm sorry that you have to stay at the tea house," said Haru. "After Lord Ohmori and his family leave, you must come and stay at the main house."

"I like the tea house, and Bunkei is good company," said Zenta. "I should be the one to apologize for troubling you at this busy time."

Haru shook her head. "Lord Ohmori is not a hard guest to serve. He is interested only in cherry blossoms, and he is not at all demanding about food or accommodations."

"Lord Ujinobu is fussy, though," said one of the maids, a plump girl with a fetching pout. "This morning the cook had to make the bean paste soup three times before it satisfied him."

"Lady Ayame is different," said the other maid, a taller and older girl.

"Who is Lady Ayame?" asked Zenta. "Lord Ohmori's daughter?"

Haru nodded. "She is very different from her brother. We have never had a single unkind word from her."

"I saw Lady Ayame practicing in the courtyard with a halberd once," said the taller maid.

Zenta was intrigued. In this age of civil wars, the women of samurai families sometimes received training in arms, although their weapon was not the sword but the halberd, a curved knife mounted on a long pole. Zenta had met a number of women warriors who were as spirited and brave as any samurai. "I wonder if Lady Ayame is good with the halberd," he murmured. He was curious to meet her.

"She must be good," said the taller maid. "She is only eighteen, but she looked as fierce as any warrior when she was practicing."

"I heard one of the samurai say that she occasionally puts on a man's clothing and goes out riding a horse!" said the plump maid.

"Lady Ayame is probably huskier than her brother," remarked Zenta. "Ujinobu didn't strike me as a robust specimen."

The plump maid giggled. "We mustn't talk like this, or we'll get into terrible trouble!"

Zenta turned to Haru. "Is Ujinobu Lord Ohmori's only son?"

Haru hesitated. "I believe so… At least Lord Ujinobu is the only one who is here with him."

Zenta wanted to ask Haru about the boy he had met, but he was reluctant to do it in front of the two talkative maids. As he waited for them to finish hanging and fluffing the quilts, his eyes went to the cherry blossoms showing like white froth above the bamboo fence. "It's a pity one of the trees over there had a branch lopped off," he said idly. "The tree in front of the tea house is ruined, too."

He was startled by the effect of his words. The two maids almost twittered with agitation, and the taller one cried, "Oh, sir it's a terrible thing! The people in our valley are convinced that our trees are doomed!"

"Is there a disease killing off the trees?" asked Zenta.

"No! Someone is deliberately mutilating the most beautiful trees!"

"Someone mutilated these trees?" exclaimed Zenta. Like all Japanese, he had a special love for the cherry blossom, and the thought that anyone could intentionally ruin such beauty was profoundly shocking to him.

"Whoever he is, he must be a fiend!" declared the taller maid.

"The people in the next valley did it," said the plump maid viciously. "They've been jealous of us for years because our trees are more famous than theirs and everyone comes here for cherry viewing."

"No, I can't believe that the people in the next valley can be so unscrupulous," said Haru.

"How long has this been going on?" asked Zenta. The vandalism had to be stopped, even if he had to do it himself.

"The tree in front of our inn was vandalized the day before yesterday," replied Haru, "and the one in front of the tea house two days earlier."

"The trees below Sairyuji Temple were damaged first," said the taller maid. "It happened the night those visitors arrived at the temple."

"I wonder if the person who damaged the trees might be con-

26

nected with the visitors." said Zenta slowly. He turned to Haru. "Do you know anything about those people?"

Haru shook her head. "No, but our guests might know. I heard some of the samurai here mention Sairyuji Temple several times. Lord Ohmori arrived about the same time as the visitors at the temple."

Zenta's interest quickened. "The vandal could also be someone in Lord Ohmori's party. Your trees have been damaged as well."

"That's not possible!" said Haru. "Lord Ohmori loves cherry trees! When he saw the damage, he was furious and offered a reward to anyone who caught the vandal. He swore he would put the guilty man to death."

"With so many men about the place, you'd think that the vandal would be captured by now," said Zenta.

Haru shook her head. "The vandal always did his work at night. We wouldn't discover the damage until next morning, and then it was too late."

"Didn't anyone at least hear a noise?" asked Zenta. It was hard to imagine how the vandal could break off a branch without making a sound.

"During the parties at our inn there is always a great deal of drinking, fighting, and dancing," said Haru. "It's so noisy here that we wouldn't hear anything outside."

"Lord Ohmori said that beginning tonight he was going to post sentries near the cherry trees," said the plump maid.

Zenta decided that the affair of the cherry trees deserved serious attention. And there was still the mystery of the strange boy. After the girls had finished hanging out the quilts, Zenta said to Haru, "Can you stay for a moment? I'd like to ask you something."

As the two maids left, Haru said, "You know that you can ask us for anything." She paused, slightly embarrassed. "If it's money that you need…"

Zenta laughed. "I don't need money. Why should I, when you provide me with free food and lodging? What I want is some information. Yesterday afternoon I met a rather unusual boy, about fourteen years old, and I wonder if you know anything about him."

"A fourteen-year-old boy? I don't think…"

"He had very thick eyebrows and rather long arms."

"Oh, I know the one you mean," said Haru. "I saw him in front of the bamboo grove one evening. He looked forlorn, and I thought he might be hungry. I offered him some food, but he ran away."

"Did he talk to you?" asked Zenta.

"Not the first time, but two days later I saw him again, this time near the tea house. When I asked him what he wanted, he said he was taking a walk because he needed the exercise."

"Then you have no idea who he is?"

"No…" Haru thought for a moment. "He didn't act like a peasant boy. Maybe he's the son of a priest or some ronin living nearby."

"And you haven't seen him since?"

"Well, he came around again yesterday while I was on my way to gather wild vegetables. I felt sorry for him, but I had a lot of work to do and couldn't stop to chat."

"You have a lot of work to do right now, and you're finding time to chat," said a sarcastic voice. The innkeeper's wife was looking at them from the kitchen step.

Haru's chin went up defiantly. "The guests are through with breakfast, and we've finished hanging out the quilts. There is nothing to do at the moment."

"Lady Ayame wants someone to mend a rip in her sleeve," said the innkeeper's wife coldly. "Do you think you can condescend to attend to her request?"

The look that Haru gave her stepmother was no less cold. Then she bowed to Zenta. "Please excuse me."

While the girl was still within earshot, the innkeeper's wife said to Zenta, "Her father spoils her. I shall have to do something about that."

"Haru has a kind heart, just like her late mother," Zenta replied.

He made the remark quite innocently, but the woman chose to be offended. A tiny line appeared between her eyebrows, marring the perfect smoothness of her face. "Not all of us can live up to Haru's sainted mother!"

Zenta was becoming tired of the woman's pettiness, and he was turning to leave when he heard her say. "You were asking Haru just now about a boy, weren't you?"

"Yes, I was," said Zenta. "Do you know anything about him?"

He felt a subtle change in her attitude toward him. Perhaps it was because he had shaved and changed into clean clothes so that he now looked less like a vagabond. More probably it was because her cousin Gonzaemon had said something to her. She still made no effort to hide her dislike, but there was less contempt in her manner. At his question she shook her head and said, "You have been warned that it is more healthy to forget about the boy's existence."

"Now, how did you know about that?" wondered Zenta. "About the warning, I mean."

For a moment she didn't answer, and Zenta took malicious pleasure in seeing her ruffled. "It doesn't matter how I know about the warning," she said finally. "Just remember that it's not healthy to inquire about him."

"Thank you very much for your concern about my health," said Zenta. He left her staring after him with narrowed eyes.

As he walked back to Bunkei's house, he marveled at how quickly news traveled. All he had done was to ask about a fourteen-year-old boy, and by next morning no less a person than the son of the local feudal lord was warning him to curb his curiosity. And no sooner had Ujinobu delivered his warning when the innkeeper's wife was repeating it in almost identical words. Someone here was a very efficient eavesdropper.

4

He was at a village festival watching the young peasant boys beating a huge drum. The strange thing was that he could feel the thuds in his head but could not hear the booming of the drum. Now the villagers were lighting the bonfire. Dancers in grotesque masks capered around the fire, jumping higher and higher. He had better step back from the fire — his face was beginning to burn.

Matsuzo opened his eyes and found that the sun was streaming down full on his face. Sitting up, he groaned aloud as the dull throb in his head became sharp and localized. Turning his head carefully, he saw that Zenta's side of the room was empty and his mattress neatly folded. Rising, Matsuzo pushed open a sliding screen and looked out. From the height of the sun, the morning seemed to be far advanced. He wondered how long Zenta had been gone.

Rather shakily, the young ronin stepped down from the veranda and splashed his face with water from the stone basin. Again a twinge of pain stabbed through his head, but when that died away he felt better. If he was as bad as this, what must Bunkei feel? The artist had drunk three times as much sake.

He found Bunkei in his room, sitting at a low desk with a brush in his hand and staring at a blank piece of paper. Ink was slowly dripping from the tip of the brush, forming a small puddle on the table but the artist didn't seem to notice.

"Oh, I didn't mean to disturb you," said Matsuzo hastily, and turned to leave.

"That's quite all right" said Bunkei. "It's no use working this morning anyway. My mood is not right." He put his brush down and dabbed absently at the pool of ink with his sleeve.

Matsuzo had expected Bunkei to have the same thundering headache as his own, but though the artist's face drooped in its usual sad scowl, he seemed quite composed. His hand as it held the brush had been rock steady. Matsuzo suddenly realized that Bunkei's hand and wrist were very muscular. The dramatic slash in Bunkei's painting required power.

"I'm afraid I drank a little too freely last night," Matsuzo admitted. "But I see that the wine hasn't affected you at all."

"I'm used to wine," said Bunkei. "Your friend drinks very sparingly doesn't he? I heard him leave this morning."

"Oh? When did he leave?"

"About an hour ago," said Bunkei. "He was gone before I had a chance to talk to him. I hope he returns soon, because I see the maids from the inn bringing breakfast."

The thought of food made Matsuzo's gorge rise but Bunkei's eyes gleamed hungrily as the maids greeted them and began to set out the trays.

The maids had hardly bowed and left when Matsuzo heard more footsteps and saw Zenta approaching. Although thin as a bamboo pole, Zenta looked fit and disgustingly cheerful as he mounted the front steps and entered the room. Matsuzo had to close his eyes for an instant. So much cheerfulness was more than he could bear.

"Ah, good!" said Zenta, sitting down and removing the lid of his soup bowl. "I'm starved."

"Where have you been?" asked Matsuzo, unable to hide a note of irritation.

"Headache?" asked Zenta sympathetically. "Never mind, drink your soup and you'll feel better."

Matsuzo picked up a piece of bean curd from his soup with his chopsticks and looked at it blearily. He almost dropped it back, but the sight of Bunkei slurping his soup with relish shamed him into eating the piece of bean curd. By the time he drank some soup and finished his first bowl of rice, he found to his surprise that he really did feel better. His headache retreated into a small corner of his head to bide its time.

Zenta popped his last piece of pickled eggplant into his mouth and put down his chopsticks. "By the way," he announced, "I've found us a job."

"Good!" said Matsuzo, delighted. "We can certainly use the money. It would be nice not to live on the innkeeper's charity any longer, especially when his wife grudges every grain of rice served to us."

Matsuzo's hopes were dashed when Zenta said, "Actually, nobody will be paying us. The job I have in mind is to discover who is mutilating the cherry trees around here."

"What?" cried Matsuzo, shocked. "You mean these crippled trees were deliberately vandalized?"

"That's true, I've heard that, too," said Bunkei. "Many in this valley would be very grateful to you if you could catch this vandal. The tree in front of my house is one of the victims."

Zenta looked curiously at Bunkei. "Didn't you hear a noise when your tree was damaged? I know that the work was always done at night but I notice that you are a light sleeper."

"I certainly would have heard the vandal if I had been at home," replied Bunkei. "But when this tree was damaged, I was away on a trip to buy an ink stick from a friend of mine."

Matsuzo couldn't imagine going on an overnight trip to buy an ink stick. "It must have been a very valuable ink stick!"

"It was," said Bunkei calmly. "The stick originally came from China, and my friend prized it highly. But he needed the money and had to sell it before even a quarter of it was used."

Zenta rose. "I'd like to go to Sairyuji Temple and look at the cherry trees there. Some of those have been mutilated as well. The abbot there knows me, and perhaps he can tell us something." He looked down at Matsuzo. "Do you feel well enough to come along?"

"Of course I'll come," declared Matsuzo. To him the beauty of nature was a gift of the gods, and wanton destruction of it was an act of desecration; the vandalism of the cherry trees aroused in him a deep sense of outrage. Pay or no pay, he was glad to help Zenta uncover the identity of the vandal.

Outside, the sun was pleasantly warm on their backs. After climbing a short distance, the two men stopped and looked back. Nestled in the valley were the inn with its thatched roof and the little bamboo grove almost hiding the yellow walls of the tea house. Here and there, puffs of cherry blossoms appeared to hang in the air like little clouds. The scene was a living landscape painting.

Zenta wondered if Bunkei ever painted conventional landscapes. He suspected that underneath Bunkei's laziness and love of comfort there was a keen intelligence. In case of need they might find a useful ally in the artist, if he could be persuaded to overcome his torpor.

Just as Zenta had remembered, the temple was a short distance up the side of the hill from the valley. Sairyuji, a Buddhist temple of the Shingon sect, had been founded in the tenth century. The temple had burned down a number of times, and most of the present buildings were less than a hundred years old.

The ronin were stopped by samurai guards at the two-story gate of the temple. Zenta was not surprised. After their experience at the inn, it was to be expected that the temple would be similarly guarded. In these violent times, every man of importance had to guard against attacks or assassination. What interested him was the fact that the guards here were also wearing the Ohmori crest.

Zenta told the guards his name and begged the favor of an interview with the abbot. In a few minutes one of the guards returned, accompanied by a young monk whom Zenta vaguely remembered from two years ago.

When Zenta introduced his companion, the young monk smiled cordially. "Please come in. The abbot is busy at the moment but he wants me to make you welcome. He will see you shortly."

Following the monk up the stone steps of the temple, Zenta looked around curiously to see if there were signs of any guests. But the place was quiet and serene. Only a few monks went about their tasks of sweeping, drawing water, and polishing the wooden corridors connecting the various buildings.

"Is it true that you have some guests staying with you?" asked Zenta.

The monk nodded. "Yes, we have, but most of them have gone to view the cherry blossoms on the eastern slopes of the hill, and we don't expect them back until late in the afternoon."

He led the two ronin into a small reception room and brought out two straw cushions for them. "The abbot is discussing scriptures with a lady who is a guest here, but he wants to see you. I hope your business with him is not urgent?"

Zenta was slightly embarrassed. "No, my business is so trivial that I shouldn't be intruding at this inconvenient time."

"Most of our guests are away, and this is a good time for your visit," said the monk. "Please excuse me for a moment. I have some orders to give in the kitchen."

The two ronin seated themselves on the cushions after the monk had left. It was very peaceful in the room. One side was completely open, and they could see the gracefully curved roof of the temple lecture hall. The dark roof, made of cypress bark, had grayish green patches of lichen, giving it a mellow look of age. A monk, wearing a dark robe of coarse hemp, was sweeping the stone path. The swishing sound he made mingled pleasantly with the liquid burst of song from a bush warbler.

Facing Zenta in the room was a pair of sliding wall panels painted in rich greens and gold. From behind the panel came the soft murmur of the abbot's voice. Now and then a woman's voice answered him, or raised slightly in question.

Matsuzo got up restlessly and went to look out a small window that faced a hill covered with cherry trees. "Look!" he suddenly exclaimed. "That tree over there has a broken branch!"

"Where? Let me see!" said Zenta. "You are right! That must be one of the vandalized trees." In his excitement he spoke more loudly than he intended.

From the next room the woman's voice said, "Who is that?"

"A young ronin and his friend who have come to call, Lady Sayo," replied the abbot's voice. "I know him from two years back."

"Let me see him," commanded the woman.

The wall panels slid apart, and the two ronin in the small reception room found themselves looking into the abbot's study. A woman was seated on a low dais in the middle of the room, while the abbot, who had opened the sliding door, still held a book of scriptures in one hand.

The abbot's clear, ageless face looked completely unchanged. He smiled at Zenta and beckoned. "Come nearer. Lady Sayo wishes to look at you."

Surprised, Zenta stared at Lady Sayo for a long moment before he finally remembered his manners. He advanced into the larger room and dropped into a deep bow. Behind him, Matsuzo followed suit.

Lady Sayo was a slender woman in her mid-thirties. She was dressed soberly but richly in a blue-gray kimono of heavy silk. Her hair, except for two shoulder-length locks framing her face, was gathered in a long, thick rope hanging straight down her back. She was not beautiful, for the bones in her face, though shapely, showed too prominently and gave her a look of harshness. Zenta had a feeling that she resembled someone he had seen. With his head lowered, he could scrutinize her hands without seeming rude. Those hands, long-fingered and very capable-looking, were also familiar.

"Tell me your names," ordered Lady Sayo.

Zenta had faced powerful warlords without quailing, but somehow this woman, with her cool, still face, made him nervous. He cleared his throat. "My name is Konishi Zenta, and my companion is Ishihara Matsuzo."

There was a little silence. Then Lady Sayo lifted a shoulder impatiently. "These are not your real names. Tell me your clan and your given names."

Zenta raised his head. "We prefer to use pseudonyms. As ronin we may find ourselves in situations that could bring discredit to our families." He meant to sound aloof and dignified, but somehow his answer came out sounding defiant.

Lady Sayo's eyes narrowed. Zenta felt them looking at him searchingly, and he tried not to fidget. Really, the woman had the ability to make him feel like a fifteen-year-old boy. Then Lady Sayo's lips twisted in amusement and she said, "Very well. You can at least tell me what you are doing here."

Zenta glanced at the abbot. "Some of the cherry trees in the valley have been mutilated, and we heard that the trees here at the temple have been damaged as well. I was hoping that the lord abbot could tell us something."

The abbot looked grave. "Yes, I've seen the damage. Unfortunately there has been no success in discovering the culprit. Whoever he is, he must be a very unhappy man, and I pray for him."

"Can you tell us which trees have been mutilated?" Zenta asked. "I'd like to inspect the damage and see if I can learn anything."

"You will do nothing about those cherry trees!" Lady Sayo broke in suddenly. "I order you to stop meddling!"

Open-mouthed with astonishment, the two ronin stared at her. The abbot's face was troubled. "Lady Sayo, don't you think…"

"I don't want to hear any more about the matter," she said sharply. She was pale with determination, and she did not look like a person who tolerated contradiction.

The abbot gave Zenta an unhappy smile. "You must come back and visit us another day. I should like to talk to you about what you have been doing in the past two years."

However friendly the manner of the abbot was, Zenta knew they were being dismissed. The two ronin bowed deeply to Lady Sayo and to the abbot, and with heads still lowered they retreated to the door.

Outside, the monk sweeping the path was still at work and the bush warbler continued its carefree song. Zenta let out his breath slowly. Groping in his sleeve, he found a piece of crumpled paper tissue and wiped his face. He glanced at his companion and found that Matsuzo was doing exactly the same thing. The two men looked at each other and both burst out laughing. The guards at the gate stared at them with chilly disapproval as they passed through.

"It's getting warm, isn't it?" said Matsuzo.

Zenta grinned. "Let's admit it: we're both frightened of that woman."

"Who is she?" asked Matsuzo.

"My guess is that she is the wife of the guest of honor at the temple, whoever he is," said Zenta.

Matsuzo frowned thoughtfully. "You know, I have a feeling that she resembles someone I've met."

"Do you think so, too?" said Zenta eagerly. "I felt that there was something about her mouth that reminded me of a person I knew. And her hands also looked familiar."

"Actually it was her eyes that reminded me of someone," said Matsuzo. "They were so cold and determined. By the way, are we going to drop our investigation of the cherry tree vandalism, as she ordered?"

"Of course not!" Zenta spoke especially firmly to show Matsuzo that he was not shaken by Lady Sayo. "I had the feeling that the abbot wanted us to find the culprit and his opinion counts more with me than Lady Sayo's."

Lady Sayo returned to her room in the temple, frowning in deep thought. Then, because she was a person who came to decisions quickly, she sent for her personal attendant. "Find me one of our household samurai," she told the girl. "I want one of our own men, not an Ohmori samurai."

When the man arrived, she said, "Two ronin came just now for a visit. If you hurry, you will find them still in sight. I want you to follow them and then report back to me within an hour on everything they do."

"What do you intend to do?" asked Matsuzo.

"Let's go up that hill first," said Zenta. "The tree we saw from the temple window must be over there."

They made their way to the back of the temple and as they went they began to hear sounds of music — the shrill piping of flutes, the dry staccato beats of the shoulder drum, and the rippling arpeggios of the zither. Curious, the two ronin quickened their steps, and when they turned over the hill, they saw spread below them the source of the merriment.

A cherry-viewing party was in progress. An area on the cherry-covered hillside had been enclosed by red-and-white-striped canvas hung vertically between posts. The canvas served as a screen to give privacy to the party of high-ranking cherry viewers, but from their slightly higher vantage point the two ronin were able to look into the enclosed area. At one end of the enclosure was a temporary stage, on which half a dozen musicians sat in a row. In front of them three girls, dressed in vibrant pink, were dancing to the music, their faces masklike under their heavy makeup. Their fluttering hands and swaying bodies vividly suggested cherry trees bending and rustling in the wind. Zenta saw that this was not a traditional folk dance of the sort enjoyed by peasants. The dainty, precise stamping of the white-stockinged feet and the crisp, pivoting turns of the dancers showed them to be highly trained performers dancing for an aristocratic audience.

The audience sat on low, reed-covered benches. On one of the front benches were three men of obviously higher rank than the rest, and Zenta recognized one of the three as Ujinobu. Next to him was an older man, whose resemblance to the younger man suggested that he was Lord Ohmori, Ujinobu's father. Slightly in front of father and son was another man, with heavy shoulders and dark brows.

At right angles to this bench was another on which was seated a lady, with two female attendants behind her. Her resemblance to Ujinobu was even more marked, and Zenta guessed that she was Lady Ayame, Lord Ohmori's daughter. He looked at her eagerly. From what the maids at the inn had said about Lady Ayame's skill in arms, Zenta had expected to find a statuesque amazon. He knew of one warlord who had a troop of women warriors taller and more muscular than most men. But this girl was slight in build. She had the same finely molded, sensitive features as Ujinobu, but whereas his indicated petulance and indecisiveness, hers suggested a character altogether more steadfast and direct. Her chin did not come to a point, as did Ujinobu's, and her eyes were wider than her brother's. She was dressed in a soft green kimono, suitable for an unmarried girl of high rank. Zenta found her beautiful.

Unconscious of what he was doing, Zenta began to descend and edge closer to the cherry-viewing party. He was drawn by the beautiful girl, the music, and the dancing. He was also curious about the man seated in front of Ujinobu and his father. Something about the man's thick eyebrows...

Through years of habit, Zenta moved quite noiselessly, but Matsuzo, mesmerized by the colorful scene below, moved less carefully. His kimono skirt brushed against some scrub bamboo, causing a rustle.

A shout rang out followed by several answering shouts. Men sprang out from the earth all around the two ronin. In an instant the peaceful hillside was bristling with armed men. Swords flashed out. "Spies! Assassins!"

"We've caught two assassins!"

Matsuzo put his hand to his sword, but Zenta seized his wrist. "No! We must show them that we're harmless."

A piece of the canvas flapped aside and Ujinobu strode out. "What is the meaning of this disturbance?"

"We caught these two men sneaking up on your cherry-viewing party, my lord," said one of the samurai. "They must be assassins."

38

"That's not true!" said Matsuzo hotly.

The stranger with the thick eyebrows emerged from the enclosure. "What is happening?" he demanded. He was followed by Lord Ohmori and the girl.

Zenta saw that Ujinobu had recognized him. "Lord Ujinobu," he said, "you talked to me at the inn this morning, and you know that my sole purpose here is to enjoy cherry blossoms and to visit the innkeeper and his daughter."

A slow smile spread over Ujinobu's sharp features. "Yes, I did see you this morning." He turned to the man with the thick eyebrows. "I felt suspicious of this man even then, my lord, and now his actions fully confirm my suspicions."

"What are you saying, Ujinobu?" cried the girl. "I know what I'm doing, Ayame," said Ujinobu. But Zenta and Matsuzo were both staring at the crest on the kimono of the man with the thick eyebrows. Several of the samurai behind him wore the same crest. It identified the man as Lord Kawai, feudal overlord of the Ohmori family. Zenta finally knew why the Ohmori family had to be accommodated at the inn: Sairyuji Temple was being occupied by Lord Kawai.

Momentarily forgetting his own danger, Zenta considered the significance of Lord Kawai's presence. Although he was not a powerful warlord in terms of men or territory, Lord Kawai controlled the vital mountain pass that opened the way to Suruga Bay. After a hundred years of civil wars, there were signs that a process of unification was beginning to take place, and the country might see peace at last under a strong leader. Unfortunately, there were at present not one but three warlords with ambitions to be the supreme leader of Japan. One of them, Takeda Shingen, had a pressing interest in Kawai territory. Although he was an immensely wealthy and powerful lord, Takeda lacked access to the sea, and possession of Lord Kawai's mountain pass would be vital to his ambitious plans.

But what was Lord Kawai doing in the domain of his vassal? Ostensibly, he had come to visit a valley famous for its cherry blossoms. Warlords, however, seldom acted from esthetic motives alone. Since the valley was an easy march to Takeda territory, was it possible that Lord Kawai was ready to negotiate and throw his support to Takeda Shingen?

Something about Lord Kawai's appearance now struck Zenta. A

closer look showed not only his thick eyebrows, but also a thick nose and full, coarse-looking lips. Zenta's eyes met Matsuzo's. They both knew where they had seen a face like that before.

Lord Kawai had apparently lost interest in the two ronin. He nodded to the circle of samurai. "Kill these two men. Then we can go back to our cherry viewing."

5
五

It was important to look calm, Zenta knew. "My lord," he said, keeping his voice level, "the abbot of Sairyuji Temple will answer for my character. He can tell you that I am no assassin."

Lady Ayame turned eagerly to her father. "Let's send a man to the temple immediately and ask the abbot if he would be so kind as to come."

"Why bother the abbot?" said Lord Kawai. "All this music and cherry viewing is too tame, and it's time for more excitement. These two ronin have the look of fighters, and I want to see how long they can last before my men finish them off." He smiled with his coarse lips and patted Lady Ayame's hand. "Don't worry. The abbot doesn't have to know anything about this."

The girl flinched away from him. For an unguarded moment, a look of disgust appeared in her beautiful dark eyes. Then she controlled her expression and turned to her brother. "You are a fool!" she told him. Again Lord Kawai signaled the circle of samurai to close in on the two ronin. "Let's have some action here!"

Zenta had already decided on a plan: he and Matsuzo must try to win their way back to the temple and seek the abbot. But first they had to break through the circle of armed men surrounding them. "Make a dash for the enclosure," he whispered to Matsuzo. "I have an idea."

After months in Zenta's company, Matsuzo didn't need further

41

directions. He knew that inside the enclosure were the stage and the benches for the spectators. These would serve as obstacles against their attackers. At Zenta's nod, the two ronin made a rush at the weak link in the surrounding circle, namely Ujinobu.

With a high yelp of fright, Ujinobu leaped aside, leaving a gap, and in the next instant the two ronin were inside the canvas enclosure.

Screaming with terror, the dancers, musicians, and female attendants scattered, some cowering behind the benches, some crawling under the cloth drapery to escape. During the momentary panic, the two ronin selected their position: they placed themselves with the stage protecting their backs and the two benches at right angles protecting their flanks.

As they faced the samurai pouring in through the gap after them, Matsuzo wondered how Zenta planned to escape from the enclosure. Although they now had a temporary breathing space, they couldn't hold out forever against such overwhelming numbers. He heard Zenta whisper, "Help me herd all the men toward that space behind the bench."

Matsuzo could not see the point of this, but decided it was not his part to question why. By now most of the attackers had crowded into the enclosure. Conditions favored the two ronin, since lack of space made it hard for the attackers to swing their swords without hurting their own men. Pushed back by Zenta's flashing sword, with Matsuzo putting pressure on the other side, the attackers became more and more tightly packed, until the majority of them were driven behind the two benches.

One man skidded on a stray flute and fell flat on the stage. His hands swept across the zither, setting up a rippling chord, and his head struck a tattoo on the drum. The resulting music was rather pleasant, thought Matsuzo. Momentarily distracted, he did not hear Zenta's whispered warning to him.

When the men had been herded into position behind the bench, Zenta raised his sword and slashed at the ropes holding up the red and white canvas. Seizing the falling cloth, he dragged it over the attackers, tripping them and wrapping them in its voluminous folds. Not all the men were trapped, but those left standing were isolated, and it was a matter of a few moments for Zenta to step over and stun them one at a time with his sword.

The scheme, like most of Zenta's schemes, was designed to create a maximum of confusion with a minimum of bloodshed. Without killing a single man, he had opened an escape route. What he had not foreseen was that Matsuzo would be equally unprepared for the falling canvas. Looking around for his companion, he found him nowhere in sight. One of these heaving shapes under the cloth, he realized with dismay was Matsuzo. But which one?

"Where are you, Matsuzo?"' he called.

A muffled voice cried out, and a hand ripped through the cloth. Zenta reached down and pulled. "Get up! We have to hurry!"

But the crimson face emerging from the cloth was that of a stranger. "Not you!" said Zenta, and struck the man down with the hilt of his sword.

Another figure staggered up, but again it was a stranger. Zenta struck him down absentmindedly and continued his search for his friend. Hearing loud laughter, he turned around and found that Lord Kawai was whooping with laughter and gasping for breath. The warlord was not bothered in the least by the discomfiture of his own men. Zenta hoped the laughter would choke him.

Standing next to Lord Kawai, Lady Ayame bit her lip, whether in anger or laughter it was impossible to say. Her father looked disgusted, but most of the disgust seemed directed at his superior. Ujinobu was close to hysteria. He shouted for more men to come, while making no move to draw his sword and come forward himself.

"I'm all right now," panted Matsuzo's voice at last. The young ronin struggled to his feet and squashed down the man next to him, who was also attempting to rise.

"We've wasted enough time!" snapped Zenta. He leaped over the prostrate, writhing bodies on the ground, closely followed by Matsuzo. Behind them they could hear some of the samurai ripping through the binding cloth, but it didn't matter. They had a head start.

But the sight ahead of them brought them up short.

Ujinobu's shouts for more men had brought results. Coming down the hillside in a solid mass were more armed men, and Zenta realized with a sinking feeling that he had miscalculated badly. He had thought that Lord Ohmori was hosting an informal cherry-viewing expedition with a retinue of some twenty or thirty men. Coming toward them in orderly ranks were at least fifty more men. Zenta turned and smiled ruefully at Matsuzo. "I'm afraid our visit to Sairyuji Temple isn't turning out the way I expected."

"Kill them! Kill them!" screamed Ujinobu's voice from below.

The soldiers in front parted ranks, and the abbot of Sairyuji Temple stepped forward. He smiled at the two ronin, saying "Sheath your swords and follow me."

Awed, Zenta bowed to the abbot. He had known that the priest was a man of great wisdom, but now it seemed that he was also gifted with second sight. Otherwise how could he have predicted that they would be in trouble and need help?

The two ronin followed the abbot back down to the shambles of the cherry-viewing party. Lord Kawai was seated once more on his bench, watching his men straightening the wooden posts and attempting to rehang the tattered canvas. When he saw the abbot he grinned. "My lord abbot, if you are coming to speak on behalf of these young men, you are too late. The havoc they've created here cannot go unpunished. I'm willing to grant them the privilege of committing hara-kiri, however, instead of having them beheaded."

Zenta's hand crept back to his sword. He had no intention of going tamely to his death, and he could see that Matsuzo felt the same.

"The havoc here is partly the work of your own men and those of Lord Ohmori," the abbot told Lord Kawai. "Would you order them to commit hara-kiri also?"

Lord Kawai's smile widened. "Why not? These men have been made to look foolish, and I have no use for fools."

The abbot's gaze swept over the cherry-covered hillside. "To carry out a mass hara-kiri ceremony under these beautiful blossoms would be in poor taste."

"I have no taste," said Lord Kawai cheerfully. "I am only a simple fighting man."

The abbot's words, however, had reached other ears. Lord Ohmori leaned over to his superior and said, "My lord, perhaps the sentence is too severe for a simple misunderstanding."

"These two men might still be assassins," said Ujinobu. "Their actions proved them to be violent."

Lady Ayame broke in. "No, their actions proved exactly the opposite. When our men were immobilized by the cloth, these ronin could easily have attacked us, if assassination had been their intention. But they did not take advantage of the opportunity." She turned to Lord Kawai. "My lord, you are not an unreasonable man. You know that these two men blundered into our party in perfect innocence."

Perhaps it was the effect of Lady Ayame's beauty, or perhaps an appeal to reason was more effective than an appeal to taste. Lord Kawai nodded. "Very well. To tell the truth, I wasn't really serious about hara-kiri. I was just curious to see everybody's reactions."

He turned to Zenta. "The entertainment you've provided was more amusing than the cherry-blossom dance. I may have a position open for someone like you."

In spite of Lord Kawai's sarcastic tone, his offer of employment appeared to be genuine. For years Zenta had existed on the edge of starvation because he was fastidious about who his employer was. Lord Kawai's personality particularly grated on him, and he was seized by a reckless impulse to say something rude. "My lord," he said, "I have only a limited talent as a court jester, and I can't promise to sustain the level of comedy you have just seen."

The amusement left Lord Kawai's face and his thick brows came down. His mouth, with its coarse lips, became cruel. After a second he said, "I can see that your brand of humor might soon become tiresome. You'd better get out of my sight before I change my mind about releasing you."

On the stage the dancers, unaware of their smeared makeup, were adjusting their kimonos. The zither player was tuning his instrument and shaking his head sadly. One of the flute players approached Lord Kawai. "My lord, shall we resume our performance?"

Lord Kawai shrugged. "Oh, very well, get on with your jiggling and jangling. But first, let's have some wine!"

As the two ronin accompanied the abbot back to the temple, Zenta said, "My lord abbot, you saved our lives by your timely arrival. But how did you guess that we'd be embroiled with the cherry-viewing party?"

"Lady Sayo told me," replied the abbot. "She said one of her men reported that you were in trouble, and she asked me to intervene."

Zenta pondered over the abbot's surprising words. He didn't know which was more astonishing: that Lady Sayo should have a man report on their movements, or that she should actively intervene to save them. Zenta found Lady Sayo's behavior inexplicable.

Matsuzo's comment echoed Zenta's thoughts: "Why should Lady Sayo go to so much trouble for us? She didn't sound very cordial when we saw her."

"Lady Sayo is not a person to show much outward warmth," chided the abbot gently. "But she was very curious about you. After you left she asked me many questions about your backgrounds."

Zenta looked at the abbot uneasily. The priest knew something of his past history, and probably guessed the rest. The thought of Lady Sayo prying into his personal affairs was an unpleasant one.

The abbot seemed to read Zenta's thoughts, and his eyes were pitying. "I didn't tell her anything you wouldn't want me to say."

"Is Lady Sayo the wife of Lord Kawai?" asked Matsuzo.

"Yes, she is," replied the abbot. "She is known for her charity to the poor and her generous contributions to various temples."

Zenta was surprised, for nothing in Lady Sayo's bearing suggested compassion. "Does she have any children?" he asked.

"Of her children, only one son has survived," said the abbot and his voice was somber.

"With parents like that, the son must be somewhat difficult," Matsuzo blurted out.

The abbot said nothing, which Zenta found ominous in itself. At the gate of Sairyuji Temple the abbot said, "Would you care to join us and share our vegetarian lunch?"

"I'm afraid we've caused you far too much trouble already," said Zenta. "We'll be returning to the inn for lunch."

The abbot made no attempt to press his invitation but gave the two ronin a kindly smile as they bowed deeply to him. They remained on their knees until he passed through the gate.

As the two men turned away from the temple, Matsuzo said, "I'm still wondering why Lady Sayo decided to help us. Do you think that in the past we performed some service for her without knowing it?"

Thinking back to Lady Sayo's searching eyes, Zenta couldn't recall any hint of gratitude in their expression. "She probably wants us to perform some service for her in the future, and is putting us under obligation to help."

"I know!" said Matsuzo. "She wants to buy our silence, in case we find out anything embarrassing about the cherry tree vandalism. Remember how she wanted to stop us from looking into the matter?"

"No, that's not the reason," said Zenta slowly. "The easiest way to prevent us from looking into the business would be to let us get killed. She went to some trouble to prevent that. No, I still think she wants us to do something for her."

He suddenly remembered that Ujinobu wanted to hire him. There was also Gonzaemon's attempt to recruit him. The valley was full of people who wanted him to do something — most likely something dishonorable.

Matsuzo stopped and pointed. "Speaking of cherry trees, I see one over there that seems to have lost a branch."

The two men walked over to the tree and inspected the damage. "I wonder if we can learn something from the cut itself," murmured Zenta, running his fingers over the stump.

"All the stumps we've seen so far have been very neat," said Matsuzo. "That means whoever did it used a saw."

After a moment Zenta shook his head regretfully. "No, I'm afraid that doesn't prove anything. The jagged end may have been trimmed off later, because a neat stump heals more easily. In order to learn anything, we have to get there right after the damage is done."

"We'll learn even more if we get there *while* it is being done," said Matsuzo.

Zenta stopped listening. For some time he had been aware that they were being followed. At first he had thought that it could be a further attack on them, but he soon dismissed the thought. Lord Kawai had no need to do anything surreptitious. Ujinobu might be malicious enough to order a secret attack. Zenta soon decided, however, that only one person was following them, and that person, while keeping his distance, was making no attempt to soften his footsteps.

Making a sign to Matsuzo for silence, Zenta sat down on a flat rock and waited. Matsuzo followed Zenta's example. "There is someone following us, isn't there?" he whispered.

Zenta nodded. Afar a few moments a figure came into sight from around a bank of the hill. Because he had been half expecting it, Zenta felt no surprise as he saw that it was the boy they had met on the previous day.

The boy's face was purposeful and when he came within five

paces of the two men he stopped and planted his feet firmly on the ground. "I want you to teach me those sword strokes you used in the fight just now," he told Zenta.

Matsuzo gave a little snort of disgust, but Zenta quelled him with a glance. He looked gravely at the boy. "Are you asking to be taken on as a pupil?"

The boy stamped impatiently. "I haven't time for that. I just want to learn a few clever tricks. Some of the strokes you used just now were good, and I want you to teach them to me."

"What is your name?" asked Zenta.

"Why do you want to know?" asked the boy suspiciously.

"I don't discuss swordsmanship with strangers," said Zenta.

The boy frowned until his thick brows made a continuous black bar across his face. "My name is Torazo," he muttered finally.

Torazo was a boyhood name. Soon it would be replaced by an adult name that would give more information on his rank and parentage. But even without any additional clue, Zenta was willing to hazard a guess about Torazo's parentage. The thick brows and the shape of the nose and mouth were unmistakable: the boy was Lord Kawai's son. Furthermore, because of Torazo's solitary state, Zenta suspected that the boy was illegitimate — not only illegitimate but unacknowledged.

Feeling a surge of pity for the slight, forlorn figure, Zenta spoke very gently. "Listen, Torazo, being a swordsman is almost a way of life. You must constantly practice many things: alertness, concentration, even proper breathing. It's not a matter of learning a few tricks."

"But I'm willing to practice!" cried Torazo, his voice cracking into a childish treble. He paused, swallowed, and brought his voice under control again. "I can work very hard, but I must have a good teacher."

"You have no teacher now?" asked Zenta.

"Of course he has one," said Matsuzo.

"I have a teacher, but I don't trust him," said Torazo.

"He probably refused to listen to the teacher," muttered Matsuzo.

Surprised and annoyed by Matsuzo's repeated interruptions, Zenta frowned darkly at him and then went back to the boy. "Do you have a particular reason for wanting to master the sword?"

"Why do you think I have to have a particular reason?" demanded Torazo. "Doesn't every samurai want to be a good swordsman?"

"You seem unusually anxious," said Zenta. He looked earnestly at the boy. "I must tell you that I won't teach you if you have some dishonorable purpose in mind."

Torazo's face darkened. "Why are you accusing me of being dishonorable? You don't want to teach me because you think I'm ugly and clumsy!"

"Ugliness I can do nothing about," said Zenta, "but clumsiness is a state of mind, and you can overcome it if you know how. You have the shoulders and arms of a swordsman, and I'm willing to teach you, but under certain conditions."

Torazo drew himself up proudly. "What are your conditions?"

"I don't know yet," said Zenta. "The conditions depend on you, and I won't be able to say what they are until I know you better."

When the boy said nothing, Zenta added, "If you decide to study with me, come to the tea house tonight at the back of the inn. We are staying with Bunkei, the artist. I think you already know where it is."

For a long moment Torazo stared, his eyes intelligent but cold. Then he turned without a word and walked rapidly away.

When the boy was out of sight Matsuzo said, "Why do you want to get involved with him? You've just refused to enter the service of Lord Kawai, and I have a strong suspicion that Torazo is his son."

"Yes, I think so, too," said Zenta. "But I don't think Lord Kawai acknowledges the boy officially."

Matsuzo looked amazed. "Not acknowledge the boy? Why shouldn't he?"

Zenta could not understand Matsuzo's impatience with Torazo. Usually his young friend was sympathetic to underdogs. "Torazo is probably Lord Kawai's son by some serving woman or entertainer," Zenta said. "That may account for his sullenness. It's understandable if he's jealous of the official heir."

"I don't know how to account for his sullenness, but it's certainly not jealousy of the official heir!" exclaimed Matsuzo. "Don't you see, Torazo is the official heir."

"That's nonsense!" said Zenta. "As Lord Kawai's heir, he wouldn't be wandering around alone. He would be surrounded by tutors for his lessons and instructors for the martial arts."

"Yes, but the Kawai family is here on a cherry-viewing expedition," Matsuzo pointed out. "Torazo must be having time off from his lessons."

"But he would still have a small retinue, or at least a trusted personal attendant," insisted Zenta. "Someone had to protect Lord Kawai's heir from being thrashed by a farmer!"

Matsuzo waved his hand with impatience. "How Torazo escaped from his attendants doesn't concern me, but he is definitely Lady Sayo's son! Didn't you notice the resemblance?"

"The only resemblance I noticed was the one to Lord Kawai," protested Zenta.

"I grant you that Torazo has Lord Kawai's thick brows and his nose and mouth," said Matsuzo. "But his eyes he got from his mother. When I first saw Lady Sayo, I felt immediately that she looked familiar. Now I understand why. Those cold eyes of hers looked exactly like Torazo's!"

Zenta was too stunned to speak, and after a pause Matsuzo said, "I wondered how you could be so carefree in offering lessons to Torazo. You didn't suspect did you, that he was Lord Kawai's only son and heir?"

6

This is a good life, thought Matsuzo. After returning from Sairyuji Temple, the two ronin had spent the rest of the day enjoying the cherry trees in the valley. They had joined Bunkei in time for dinner, a delicious meal featuring tiny freshwater fish, which were a specialty of the region. Matsuzo's back still tingled pleasantly from its vigorous scrubbing by a pretty serving girl during his predinner bath. Haru and her father, while busily serving the Ohmori family, did not neglect the comforts of the guests in the tea house.

Matsuzo was interested to observe a change in the attitude of the innkeeper's wife. When the two ronin saw her after they emerged from the bathhouse, she greeted them less glacially than before, although there was still no friendliness in her stiff smile. What had changed her manner toward them? Perhaps Lady Ayame had said a good word for them. Matsuzo recalled that she had defended them after the fight. Lady Ayame was beautiful and well disposed toward them, but there was a hint of stubbornness in her jaw which he found unattractive. Zenta, on the other hand, admired women with spirit. Matsuzo hoped that he would not be attracted to Lady Ayame, for the consequences could be disastrous.

But now, with the dinner comfortably settled in his stomach, Matsuzo was not seriously worried about anything. Outside, the rain fell steadily — a gentle spring rain, not the relentless summer rain which could last for days. Tomorrow could very well be a fine day

51

again. He stretched out on the tatami mat and watched Bunkei rubbing an ink stick on a small stone slab. It made a low, regular grinding noise very soothing against the patter of the rain. Matsuzo yawned. It was still early in the evening, but he was already sleepy from the effect of the mild spring air.

In another corner of the room Zenta was polishing his swords. "I wonder if Torazo will come?" he said.

Bunkei picked up a brush to test the blackness of the ink but put it down again. "So you really think the boy is Lord Kawai's son?"

Zenta had told Bunkei about their visit to the temple and the events that followed. He had confessed to Matsuzo that he found Bunkei's paintings incomprehensible, but he believed that the artist had a sharp eye. Bunkei knew a great deal about the affairs of the valley and his opinions would be useful.

"Torazo's resemblance to Lord Kawai is unmistakable," said Zenta. "Matsuzo says that he can also detect a resemblance to Lady Sayo, although I don't find it too obvious myself."

"If Lady Sayo is Torazo's mother, that would explain why she asked the abbot to help us," Matsuzo pointed out. "Torazo must have told her that we saved him from a savage beating."

"Torazo didn't look like the type of boy who would confide such a thing to his mother," Zenta said stubbornly. "There is another thing puzzling me. If Torazo is the official heir why does he seem so unhappy?"

Absently, Bunkei dried his smudged fingers by running them through his hair. "I've heard some gossip recently that may have something to do with all this."

He paused, got up, and peered into the hallway and then out the window. "I want to make sure that Gonzaemon is not lurking outside eavesdropping on us," he said. Satisfied that no one was outside he sat down again and continued. "One of my friends, who is painting some panels for Lord Ohmori..." Bunkei's voice trailed off, and his face became thoughtful. "Now, why did *he* get the commission? His technique is passable, but his ideas are so trite..."

By now Matsuzo had learned that when Bunkei stared discussing art he could go on for hours. "What did your friend tell you about Lord Ohmori?" he prompted.

"Ah, yes," said Bunkei. "Well, he has heard that Lord Ohmori and

Lord Kawai have a serious disagreement. It's a question of who they think will emerge as the dominant warlord in the country, you see. Lord Ohmori believes that it will be Takeda Shingen, and he wants his master to join the Takeda camp. But Lord Kawai refuses. He wants to wait and see."

Zenta grunted. "I can understand Takeda's interest in acquiring Kawai territory, since it would open the way to the seacoast that he lacks. Then you think Lord Ohmori might desert his overlord and go over to Takeda Shingen?'

Bunkei nodded. "Mind you, this is just a rumor which my friend has heard through a serving woman. If anyone hears us discussing this we could all lose our heads."

"Then isn't Lord Kawai taking a dangerous risk by coming to the cherry-viewing party in the middle of Ohmori territory?" objected Zenta. "You talk about losing heads. Lord Ohmori might kill Lord Kawai and present his head as a gift to Takeda Shingen."

Bunkei pursed his lips. "There is another rumor, that Lord Kawai has fallen in love with Lady Ayame." Zenta frowned. "Yes, I think I've seen signs."

"Because of his infatuation he may be acting more rashly than he usually does," said Bunkei. "Since he cannot take a girl of her rank as a concubine, it is possible that he will offer to marry her. With Lady Ayame installed as Lord Kawai's wife, her father will probably overcome his temptation to defect. No doubt Lord Kawai thought this would guarantee his safety when he accepted the cherry-viewing invitation."

To Matsuzo's alarm, Zenta's lips tightened — he was interested in the girl, after all. But Zenta's next remark was not about Lady Ayame at all. "What does Lady Sayo say to the proposed marriage of her husband? Surely your well-informed friend knows something about this also?"

Bunkei waved his inky fingers negligently. "I don't imagine Lady Sayo would be too unhappy. She is said to be contemplating a religious life, anyway, and would be glad to retire to a nunnery, provided her husband endows it handsomely."

Even Matsuzo saw the next difficulty. "Lady Sayo might be willing to retire in favor of a younger successor, but she might not like the idea of her son supplanted by an offspring produced by the second marriage."

This was a possible explanation for Torazo's unhappiness, Matsuzo thought. Already the boy was troubled by his ugliness and clumsiness. And now there was a good chance that he might be set aside from the succession. If Lady Ayame married his father and bore him a son, Torazo would be supplanted as the heir, and his future would be a bleak one. Being the older son, he would always pose a threat. The usual solution in such a case would be to force him to become a monk. If he refused, he might even be imprisoned. His very life might be in danger, for a convenient assassination could always be arranged.

Zenta gave his swords a final polish with a soft cloth and sheathed them with almost maternal care. "We're indulging in too much guesswork. It's possible that we're entirely wrong."

In the silence that followed, they realized that the rain had stopped, and they could hear music coming from a party at the inn. Suddenly there was a shout, followed by the sound of running. Zenta jumped up and pushed open a panel of the outer wall. "Could that be Torazo? Perhaps he has decided to come after all." He ran out in the direction of the cherry grove.

In a few moments Matsuzo heard more shouts, and they sounded angry. "Zenta may need help," he said, and dashed out.

The ground squelched under his feet, but he paid no heed, for he could see lanterns and torches bobbing up and down ahead of him as men poured out of the inn toward the clearing with the cherry trees. Suddenly he slipped and pitched forward into the muddy ground. When he tried to sit up, his right leg felt as if it were on fire, and he hissed with pain. His groping hands found his shin scraped raw, and he realized that what had tripped him was a thick stick. But when he picked up the stick, he discovered that it was a branch from a cherry tree.

Before he could recover from his surprise, rough hands seized him, and a voice shouted, "We've got him! We caught the vandal right in the act!"

"Now, wait…" protested Matsuzo, struggling. "He's trying to escape! Don't let him get away!"

"Look, I tripped over this branch…" began Matsuzo.

More men ran up. Matsuzo's arms were tightly bound behind his back and he was dragged to the clearing. Lord Ohmori and Ujinobu were standing and staring at one of the cherry trees.

At the sight of the tree Matsuzo momentarily forgot his own danger. It was the biggest tree of the group, and it had had the loveliest shape. Now, with one of its main limbs broken off, the shape was ruined forever. It had taken a few vicious blows for the vandal to destroy a beautiful tree more than a hundred years old. In the torchlight, Lord Ohmori's eyes glistened with tears.

"My lord, we've caught the culprit!" said Matsuzo's captors and threw him down in front of their master.

Lord Ohmori stared down at the young ronin. Then he drew back his arm and struck Matsuzo a vicious blow across the face. "I'll see that you pay for this!"

"You are making a mistake, my lord," said Matsuzo, through lips which were beginning to swell. But he realized that he did not present a prepossessing sight. There was mud from his fall all over his face and down the front of his kimono.

One of the men waved the broken branch. "He was still clutching this when we captured him!"

"Listen, I just tripped over the cherry branch," said Matsuzo desperately. "It could easily have happened to one of your own men."

Lord Ohmori gave no sign of having heard him. He turned to one of his samurai. "You, there! This morning you said you wanted to test a new sword. Here is your chance."

Matsuzo's chest tightened. They were going to execute him without giving him a chance to explain! What a stupid way to die! He looked around and saw no sign of Zenta. That was his sole comfort. At least Zenta was safely out of this.

One of the samurai suddenly cried, "I recognize this man now! He is one of the two ronin we saw this morning!"

"Hah! I knew they were scoundrels!" said another man.

"Where is the second man?' demanded someone.

A silence fell over the crowd, and a voice said out of the darkness, "I'm over here."

It came from above them. A dozen torches were instantly raised, and their light showed Zenta standing on the flight of stone steps going up to the small hill overlooking the clearing. He descended the steps unhurriedly. "You can get a good view from up there. While you were all busily capturing the wrong man, I saw some-

55

body running away."

"Seize him!" thundered Lord Ohmori.

Zenta made no effort whatever to resist. "If you weren't so excited, you would soon see why neither of us could be the vandal," he said.

Matsuzo was almost choking with anger at Zenta. "Why did you come back? If you had got away, you could have found the real culprit and cleared my name. Now both of us will die from this stupid mistake!"

"Neither of us will die from this stupid mistake," said Zenta, speaking quietly. Matsuzo finally realized that Zenta was making every effort to remain calm, and he was trying to project his calmness to the Ohmori men.

He was succeeding, for the mood of the crowd was now noticeably less hysterical. "He could be right, you know," said one man. "Maybe we were a little hasty."

Another man said, "That's true. A guilty man would not have come back."

Lord Ohmori, however, was beyond reason. "We are wasting time! Kill them! Kill both of them!"

"The mutilation of the cherry trees began last week, didn't it?" asked Zenta. By deliberately pitching his voice low, he forced the others to quiet down. "We only arrived yesterday afternoon."

"That's true!" The cry came from Haru. She pushed herself forward from the ranks of the samurai and knelt down in front of Lord Ohmori. "These two gentlemen arrived here long after the vandalism started. They are good men, my lord. They couldn't possibly be responsible for the damage."

"They say they only arrived yesterday," said Lord Ohmori stubbornly. "But they could have been hiding around here for weeks!"

Zenta was examining the crippled tree. "Look at the fresh wound on this tree, my lord. You can see a small strip of bark torn off. The vandal didn't have time to chop all the way through, and he ended by breaking the branch off and tearing a bit of the bark. Since the torn strip of bark is on the *top* of the branch, it means the blows were aimed from below. If I were to do it, I would have to stoop. My friend is also too tall to deliver the blows standing upright."

There was a small gasp. It came from Lady Ayame, who had

arrived unnoticed. Matsuzo saw that she was nodding vigorously, her eyes shining with approval.

"He's right" said a voice from the crowd. "The culprit must be someone quite a bit shorter."

Lord Ohmori was still frowning. He refused to accept the fact that there was no one he could immediately punish. Further support for the two ronin came from a most unexpected source. Ujinobu stepped forward. "Father, I believe that these men really are innocent. We should release them."

Lord Ohmori looked puzzled. "But Ujinobu, only this morning you said you distrusted them. You even called them assassins!"

Matsuzo saw that Ujinobu was looking at them. There was not a trace of friendliness in the glance. "I admit that I found these ronin insolent," said Ujinobu. "But that doesn't alter the evidence. Whoever broke this cherry branch had to strike the blows from below. A tall man would have to stoop, and it would have been very awkward for him."

There was no doubt that Ujinobu's opinion weighed with Lord Ohmori. "Very well," he said. "Have these men released. I know you don't like them. Therefore, if you ask for their release, I must believe that they're innocent."

As men came forward to untie the two prisoners, Lady Ayame said, "Father why don't we enlist these ronin to search for the real vandal? They've shown themselves to be observant and resourceful."

Lord Ohmori looked annoyed. "Really, Ayame, we have enough men of our own."

"Ayame's idea may be a good one, Father," said Ujinobu. "Our men are needed for guard duty, whereas these ronin can go all over the valley and search for the vandals."

"Do as you wish, then," said Lord Ohmori indifferently. He turned for a last look at the crippled tree. "So much beauty destroyed. If I ever find the criminal who did this, I'll make him suffer!"

After Lord Ohmori and his family had left, Matsuzo smiled painfully at Zenta. "You know, I'm beginning to think that I've had enough of cherry blossoms. There are other nice flowers — wild azaleas and peonies, for example." His lips were swollen from Lord Ohmori's blow, his scraped shin burned, and his arms ached as circulation was restored. He knew that he looked even worse than he felt.

Zenta ignored Matsuzo's banter. Absently rubbing his wrists, he stood deep in thought. One of the Ohmori samurai approached. "Here are your swords. If you will spare a moment, Lord Ujinobu wishes to see you." His manner was considerably more respectful than before. Apparently they were no longer suspicious characters but future Ohmori retainers carrying the recommendation and possibly even the favor of their young master.

The first person they saw when they entered the inn was Haru. She flashed them a radiant smile. "I'm so glad everything has turned out well," she said as she hurried off with a tray of sake bottles.

The two ronin were conducted to one of the principal rooms of the inn. Partitions had been removed to form one large hall. Evidently a drinking party had been in progress, until interrupted by the alarm over the cherry tree, for the cushions for the guests and the trays of food were still in place. When the two ronin entered, the guests were seating themselves and chattering noisily.

The seat of honor was empty, and Matsuzo guessed that Lord Ohmori was too disturbed by the destruction of the cherry tree to continue with the party. Instead, Lady Ayame sat on a cushion to one side of Lord Ohmori's empty place. A well-bred lady could not drink with the men, but she evidently wanted to hear everything that passed.

On seeing the two newcomers, Ujinobu invited them to sit at the end of the room, where two additional cushions had been placed on the floor for them. As the serving girls went around to pour wine for the guests, a musician approached Ujinobu. "My lord, would it please you to have the dancer again?"

Ujinobu waved him away. "No, that's enough for tonight. We want to talk." He turned to Zenta. "As you've gathered, our family is prepared to offer a handsome reward to anyone who discovers the cherry tree vandal. Now, I'm so certain you will find the criminal that I shall have the reward money sent immediately to the tea house for you." He paused. "In fact, it may be a good idea for both of you to move into the inn. Then you can report to me more easily."

Zenta had already attacked the food in front of him as if it were the first meal of the day. At Ujinobu's words, he put down his chopsticks and bowed. "You are too generous, my lord. I'm also appalled by the mutilation of the trees, and I shall gladly work to discover the vandal without accepting any payment." He looked around and met the eyes of the innkeeper's wife, who was supervising the serving girls. "Nor can we possibly move our quarters to the inn. I have it on good authority that the inn is completely full."

Matsuzo nearly dropped his wine cup in dismay. Why was Zenta going out of his way to rebuff Ujinobu? And what was wrong, anyway, with receiving money for investigating the cherry tree vandalism? During the past months, Zenta had accepted money from a variety of people, including even a merchant who had hired them as bodyguards.

Ujinobu looked as if he could not believe his ears. "Well!" he sputtered. No trace of the artificial graciousness was left on his face, which now assumed its more natural expression of malice and petulance. "You seem to forget that I saved your lives just now!"

Zenta looked as unmoved by Ujinobu's graciousness as by his anger. "We owe our lives to a number of people already. Only this morning, when you called us assassins, the abbot of Sairyuji Temple had to intervene to save us."

At last Matsuzo understood Zenta's refusal to become a henchman of the Ohmori family. Their position was an awkward one. On the one hand, the abbot, prompted by Lady Sayo, had saved them that morning. On the other hand, Lady Ayame and Ujinobu had spoken up for them just now. If there was any truth to Bunkei's gossip, then a conflict might develop between Lady Sayo and the Ohmoris over the future of her son, Torazo. Since he and Zenta were equally obligated to both sides, Matsuzo now saw that they could not join either.

Zenta's words infuriated Ujinobu. He pounded his fist on the floor, causing his wine cup to bounce out of his tray. "So! You're blaming me for calling you assassins!"

"That's a misunderstanding we should all forget," said Lady Ayame. She did not raise her voice, but her tone was firm, and it had the desired effect. Ujinobu subsided, still muttering angrily.

Matsuzo began to share Zenta's admiration for Lady Ayame. Besides beauty, she had warmth and humanity. She was also intelligent. It was a pity that she was a woman, for the future of the Ohmori family would surely be better in her hands than in the hands of the weak and spiteful Ujinobu. Marriage to Lord Kawai, however, would not provide real scope for her abilities. That warlord did not look like a man who would accept advice from his wife, and after her marriage Lady Ayame's future would be largely decorative.

"Tell me," Lady Ayame said to Zenta, "you mentioned earlier that you saw someone running away from the clearing with the cherry trees. Could you see who it was?"

Zenta looked at her in silence for a moment. Then he said, "No, it was too dark for me to make out the person's features."

Lady Ayame looked disappointed. "What a pity. You can't even say anything about the man's general physique or size?"

Again Zenta hesitated. Finally he said slowly, "I thought for a moment that the figure resembled Gonzaemon."

The innkeeper's wife rushed forward and threw herself down in front of Ujinobu. "No! He's lying!"

Ujinobu looked from the frantic woman to Zenta, and then to his sister. On his face was a mixture of anger and confusion, plus a hint of something else. Was it nervousness? Suddenly he jumped to his feet and sent his tray flying in a shower of bottles, cups, chopsticks, and tiny dishes. Without a word he pushed past the bewildered serving girls and out of the room.

Lady Ayame rose more slowly. She arranged her trailing skirt behind her and nodded calmly to the company before she followed her brother from the room.

Matsuzo turned and looked at his companion. "What was that all about?"

Zenta shook his head and put down his chopsticks. "I have no idea. But from the look of things, Ujinobu has changed his mind about hiring us as investigators of the cherry tree vandalism. We'll have to do the job without pay."

7

The earth smelled wet, and the branches of the cherry trees were weighted down with moisture. The ground under the trees was white with petals beaten down by last night's rain. How short-lived the blossoms were, thought Matsuzo, as he and Zenta climbed up the hill to Sairyuji Temple. A wave of melancholy went through him at the impermanence of beauty, and he groped for words to express his feeling in poetry.

In the distance, the slow-paced mellow booms of the Sairyuji Temple bell tolled the Hour of the Snake. The morning was not far advanced, then. Instead of composing his own poem, the words that ran through Matsuzo's head were the opening lines of *Tale of the Heike:* "The sound of the bell of Jetavana echoes the impermanence of all things."

"Composing a poem to the cherry blossoms?" asked Zenta. Apparently he could always tell when Matsuzo was in the grip of poetry.

Matsuzo grinned ruefully. "I was struck by the short life of the blossoms, and I wanted to put the thought into words. But somebody else has already said it better."

"The life of the cherry blossom is even shorter when someone breaks the branch off," said Zenta dryly.

And that brought back the bewildering events of the previous night. Zenta had not been talkative when they returned to the tea house, and it was Matsuzo who had satisfied Bunkei's curiosity about the uproar. The artist had stayed home — he was hard at work and didn't want to put down his brush, he said. He had even shown them the fruit of his concentration: a painting with two series of squiggles, the product of forty years of training. It had briefly crossed Matsuzo's mind that Bunkei might be a physical coward, but he soon dismissed the thought as unworthy. Artists, when engaged in creative activity, hated to be interrupted.

Zenta had returned early to his room, where he sat motionless for most of the evening. He needed to think, he had said. Matsuzo and Bunkei had discussed art, or rather Bunkei had expounded while Matsuzo listened enthralled. Since Gonzaemon had not supplied any sake, the evening had been a sober one.

The thought of Gonzaemon recalled a puzzling incident. Matsuzo glanced at Zenta, who was walking steadily ahead, still silent and thoughtful. "Did you really see Gonzaemon running away last night?" asked the young ronin.

"I'm pretty sure it was Gonzaemon," said Zenta slowly. "The funny part of it was that he was running toward the inn when I saw him."

"Do you think he had anything to do with the vandalism?"

Zenta shook his head. "I simply don't know. If he did, he had to stoop down or squat to chop at the tree. Can you think of any reason why he should do that?"

Matsuzo couldn't. He couldn't think of any reason why Gonzaemon should chop at the tree at all. He still thought the vandalism was the work of a madman, and Gonzaemon didn't seem to be mad — mysterious, but not mad. "The innkeeper's wife was upset when you said you saw Gonzaemon," he said, smiling at the memory.

"She certainly was concerned about her cousin," said Zenta. "If he really is her cousin, and I have some doubts about that."

As the massive gate of Sairyuji Temple came into view, Matsuzo began to feel qualms. "Are you sure it's a good idea to come? We didn't make ourselves very popular yesterday."

"We are here for a perfectly respectable reason," said Zenta. "We have come to thank Lady Sayo for saving our lives. If they don't like us, they can simply shut the gate in our faces."

But the guard at the gate seemed friendly enough. "Hey, look! It's those two young troublemakers again!" The man was wearing the Kawai insignia. He called to some of the Ohmori samurai stationed in the temple courtyard. "Don't let them trip you up with canvas again!"

Matsuzo remembered that most of the men who had been entangled in the folds of the canvas were Ohmori men. This fact seemed to amuse the Kawai samurai, and he readily agreed to convey the thanks of the two ronin to his mistress. In a short time he returned with the message that Lady Sayo wanted to see them immediately.

When Matsuzo followed Zenta through the small side door in the gatehouse, he noticed that the grounds of the temple were now bustling with men, and the peace and quiet he had enjoyed so much were gone. Much of the activity centered around a small square pavilion with three open sides and a wall painted with a pine tree on the fourth side. With rising excitement Matsuzo recognized the building as an outdoor Noh stage.

"Are you having a performance of Noh here?" he asked.

"Yes, there is one planned for tomorrow afternoon," said the samurai. "Lord Ohmori engaged a troupe of Noh actors especially to entertain our lord. The leading actor is a favorite of Lord Ohmori, and he is said to be outstanding."

Matsuzo looked back at the stage wistfully. He was a devoted admirer of the Noh stage, and knew many scenes from the more famous plays by heart. He wondered if there was some way in which he and Zenta could attend the performance. It was a pity that they were out of favor with both Lord Kawai and Lord Ohmori. Perhaps a friendly monk at the temple could find an inconspicuous corner where they could sit and watch the performance.

They found Lady Sayo in a small reception room opened to a landscaped garden, where cushions of moss sparkled with moisture and rocks, with patches of yellow lichen, looked hoary with age. Upon the entrance of the two ronin, Lady Sayo dismissed her female attendant.

The two men bowed down until their heads nearly touched the floor. "We thank you for calling the abbot's attention to our danger and saving our lives," said Zenta.

Lady Sayo looked faintly amused. "My lord said it was the best entertainment he has had since arriving in the village."

"I'm glad he enjoyed himself," murmured Zenta.

Lady Sayo gave him a sharp look. "But he wasn't too pleased

when you spurned his offer to take you into his service." When Zenta merely bowed once again without answering, she asked curiously, "What are your plans?"

She had saved their lives — for whatever reason of her own — and she deserved a truthful answer. "We came here to enjoy the cherry blossoms," said Zenta, "and we have no plans beyond spending a few pleasant days with the artist Bunkei in his tea house."

Matsuzo became aware that Lady Sayo was looking at Zenta with a strange intensity. For a horrible moment he entertained the notion that she might be falling in love with Zenta. But that was impossible. She was at least ten years older than he was, and she did not have the look of a person in love. She certainly appeared to be very curious about him, however.

Zenta raised his head. "Lady Sayo, please excuse my presumption. May I ask if your son's name is Torazo?"

Lady Sayo's eyes widened. "Yes, it is. Why do you ask?"

"We've met him — twice, in fact," replied Zenta. "Does he often go out without his attendant? It doesn't seem very safe."

Lady Sayo became expressionless. Without a trace of human warmth, her thin, bony face looked forbidding. She remained silent for so long that Matsuzo thought she disdained to answer Zenta's question. Finally she said levelly, "Torazo is a moody boy, but it's a passing stage and he will grow out of it eventually." There was no affection in Lady Sayo's voice, only impatience. For the first time since he set eyes on that unattractive boy, Matsuzo began to feel sorry for him.

"Does your son have a good fencing instructor?" asked Zenta.

"Of course he does," said Lady Sayo, obviously startled by the abrupt change of subject. "My lord insisted on hiring a renowned swordsman."

"Your son said that he distrusted his teacher," said Zenta.

Lady Sayo's surprise looked genuine. "Torazo is not making good progress with the sword. He is naturally clumsy. His father is very displeased, but there is no reason to distrust the instructor, for he certainly did his best with Torazo."

"Torazo evidently doesn't believe that," said Zenta. "He has asked me to be his teacher."

Matsuzo expected to see Lady Sayo seriously offended. For Torazo

64

to spurn the renowned teacher hired by his father and approach an unknown ronin was a grave affront. Lady Sayo's reaction caught Matsuzo by surprise. She looked pleased. "I have tried many things with Torazo without success. If you can teach him swordsmanship, you will not find me ungrateful."

Zenta appeared to be surprised by Lady Sayo's reaction as well. After a moment he collected himself and bowed. "Torazo may have changed his mind about wanting me as his teacher. I haven't seen him since he first spoke to me."

"Then let us send for him and hear what he has to say," decided Lady Sayo. She clapped for the attendant. But when the woman returned from seeking Torazo, she reported that he was nowhere to be found. Next the boy's personal attendant was sent for. He was an elderly samurai, dignified but very nervous, and Matsuzo suspected that he had been appointed because he was an old family retainer and not because he had any real ability. Upon being questioned about Torazo's disappearance he became so agitated that it was clear the boy had long ago grown out of his control. Matsuzo was relieved when the man was dismissed and the embarrassing scene ended.

As the two ronin walked down the hill back to the inn, Matsuzo thought about Lady Sayo's indifference when she questioned the old retainer. "What a coldhearted woman! She didn't seem to care what happened to her son."

"She may be worried," said Zenta, "and only pretending that Torazo's disappearance is of no importance."

Matsuzo suddenly remembered something the abbot had said earlier, that Lady Sayo seldom showed outward warmth. Perhaps she was not really as indifferent as she sounded. It was hardly proper to accuse her of cold-heartedness, especially when she had taken the trouble to save them only yesterday. The young ronin began to feel slightly ashamed.

"Do you think we should have warned Lady Sayo about the danger of Lord Ohmori betraying his master?" he asked Zenta. "Lord Kawai and his family could be in danger."

Zenta shook his head. "We can't repeat a rumor which we heard third hand. If it reached Lord Kawai's ear, it could cause a breach when there had been none before. The Ohmori family would be ruined."

"What happens to the Ohmori family is no concern of ours," said Matsuzo. "We don't owe them anything,"

"But we do! Lady Ayame saved our lives, and we are under obligation to her."

So they were! Matsuzo nearly groaned aloud with annoyance. Matters were so complicated that they could not move a step in this valley without bumping into one of their obligations.

He soon became aware of footsteps behind them, and he suspected that remaining neutral would be hard, if not impossible. The two men stopped, and neither was surprised when their pursuer came in sight and revealed himself to be Torazo.

The boy gave them a sketchy bow. "I've decided to take lessons from you," he announced to Zenta.

Now that Matsuzo was certain of Torazo's parentage, he could see more clearly the resemblance to both Lord Kawai and Lady Sayo. But there was also an important difference. Whereas both his parents had taken their superiority for granted, Torazo seemed insecure. As he made his announcement to Zenta, he looked unsure of his reception and defiant at the same time.

Zenta merely nodded pleasantly. "Very well. Come along then."

Torazo's shoulders sagged with relief. As they walked, he said, "I meant to come last night, but I was prevented."

"Last night was not a good time for a lesson, anyway," said Zenta. "We were all busy here."

"That's what I heard," said Torazo, smiling faintly. Matsuzo had not found the events of the previous evening very amusing — his scraped shin still hurt. It would seem that the boy had the same sort of humor as his father.

"Are we going to start the lessons right now?" Torazo asked Zenta.

"No," said Zenta. "We're going to Bunkei's house to eat lunch first."

Torazo opened his mouth to protest, but shut it again. Matsuzo wondered at his reluctance to take the time even for lunch. In any normal boy, it could be simply impatience to begin a new game. But Torazo was clearly not a normal boy.

Bunkei was on the point of beginning his lunch when they arrived. This time the trays had not been brought by the maids, but by Haru herself. She beamed at the new arrivals. "Since we are less busy

66

at the inn today, I have a moment to visit you." Her eyes widened at the sight of Torazo.

The boy stepped forward and bowed. "I'm Torazo." He had apparently decided not to announce his rank. Matsuzo was relieved, for the atmosphere in Bunkei's house was easy and relaxed, and it would be spoiled if the boy were to stand on his dignity.

Haru's friendly smile included Torazo. "I'll bring some food for you, too," she told him.

"I've eaten already," said Torazo.

"You can always eat more," she assured him, and went off before he could protest.

Zenta sat in his usual place and pulled up a tray. "Where is Gonzaemon?" he asked.

Bunkei took a sip of his soup before answering. "Off on one of his errands, probably. Even when he's engaged in something perfectly innocent, he makes it sound mysterious. But he did say that he would be back later with some sake."

At the mention of Gonzaemon, Torazo's eyes flickered, but he quickly looked down. Matsuzo noticed that the boy was tense. When Haru appeared with another tray, he pushed it aside brusquely. "I told you I'm not hungry!"

"All right," said Haru, unruffled. "But I'll leave the tray here in case you want to eat later." She bowed and left.

Torazo seemed consumed with nervousness. When Zenta accepted yet another bowl of rice from Bunkei, the boy jumped up and walked over to a window. He stood looking out, almost palpitating with impatience to be gone.

Zenta finally put down his chopsticks. "If you're ready, we'll go ask Haru for two sticks to use as practice swords," he told Torazo.

At Zenta's words, Torazo whipped around, his face pale and set. "I want to go away from here. I don't want a lot of people crowding around and staring at me."

"Of course," said Zenta calmly. "We'll look for a quiet clearing with privacy."

After Zenta left with the boy, Matsuzo and Bunkei finished their lunch at leisure. "This food is too good to be hurried over," remarked the artist. "But I wish we had some sake to go with it. What is keeping Gonzaemon?"

They did not have long to wait. The door opened, and Gonzaemon's face appeared, sweeping the room with his dazzling smile and his bright, inquiring gaze. "What, only two of you? Where is Zenta?" He brought in a huge earthenware jug and some cups.

Matsuzo found the man's curiosity irritating and saw no reason why he should gratify it. "Zenta had to leave early," he said shortly.

"Oh? What is he doing?"

"He doesn't have to account for his actions," snapped Matsuzo. "We don't ask, for instance, what you were doing last night, during the height of the uproar over the cherry trees."

To Matsuzo's disappointment, Gonzaemon showed no trace of alarm. His bright smile became a positive smirk. "But I don't mind telling you. I was visiting my cousin, and we discussed family affairs."

Bunkei gave a snort of disgust. "Enough of this. Is your sake any good or not?"

Gonzaemon lifted the jug and poured. "Of course it's good. My cousin gives me nothing but the best wine."

He was not lying about the wine, at least. The sake was superb, and Matsuzo and Bunkei emptied their cups in appreciative silence. As Gonzaemon tilted the jug again, he said, "I see that there is a fourth tray here. Did someone else come?"

Again annoyed by this persistent curiosity, Matsuzo said nothing. Bunkei answered, "Yes, it was the young boy, the one Zenta was inquiring about. Haru brought him some food, but he didn't stay to eat it."

Gonzaemon looked thoughtfully at the tray, and then at Zenta's empty place. Without his usual smile, Matsuzo noticed, his face was somewhat hard. Suddenly he rose. "I have some errands. Please excuse me."

When the door closed after Gonzaemon, Bunkei said, "More of his mysterious errands." He poured generous servings of sake into their cups. "Drink up. There's plenty here."

Matsuzo looked at the huge jug dubiously. "We can't finish this all by ourselves. There are only two of us!"

"Even if Zenta were here, he wouldn't make much difference," Bunkei pointed out, emptying his cup. "He's a very moderate drinker, isn't he? Don't you find it hard to live up to his standards all the time?"

It nettled Matsuzo to hear anything approaching criticism of his friend. "Zenta doesn't tolerate carelessness about the sword, and he believes that too much wine spoils his concentration."

"Well, we can't all be samurai," said Bunkei comfortably.

"But you have high standards when it comes to art, don't you?" asked Matsuzo. "You wouldn't tolerate any slipshod work in painting!"

Bunkei seemed struck by this observation. "That's true! I don't!" Then he poured more sake. "Fortunately, I'm not working at the moment, and I can drink all I want."

Although he was not working, Bunkei seemed quite ready to talk about art. Matsuzo sipped his wine as he listened to the artist comparing the techniques of various schools of painting currently in fashion. But for some reason the young ronin found himself drinking less freely than before. Perhaps it was the thought of Zenta hard at work with Torazo somewhere outside while he himself was lolling at his ease in the tea house. Since Matsuzo didn't want to hurt Bunkei's feelings by refusing wine, he pretended to be drunker than he was. Soon he lay back and closed his eyes.

Bunkei evidently found it less interesting to drink alone, for he got up after a while and stretched. Through slitted eyes Matsuzo watched the artist yawn, push open a panel, and step outside. A minute later he heard the sound of Bunkei's steps receding into the distance.

It was peaceful in the tea house. Relaxed by the wine and the good food, Matsuzo was content to lie still and think about nothing in particular. This was already their third day in the valley, and he should make another attempt to compose a poem in honor of the cherry blossoms. But he felt too languid to make the effort. After a hard winter, it was good to know they had soft mattresses spread out for them every night and delicious meals punctually served. The thought gave him a twinge of guilt: Haru had the burden of looking after Bunkei and the two ronin, in addition to her guests at the inn. All this luxury was spoiling him.

He was just about to rouse himself to activity when he heard voices. This time it was not Bunkei. To his amazement, it sounded like Ujinobu speaking to someone outside the window. Matsuzo could recognize that slightly nasal voice anywhere.

"It's safe to talk here. There is no one except the younger of the two ronin, and he is sleeping off the wine. We don't have to worry about being overheard."

Ujinobu's voice was quite close. He was probably standing just beyond the veranda. Matsuzo decided to lie very still, and he gave a snore to add color.

"We've chosen you to perform the deed because you owe your present standing entirely to the patronage of our family," said Ujinobu. "This is your chance to show your gratitude."

"Yes, I owe everything to Lord Ohmori," said the other man. He had a beautiful voice, sonorous even when soft. It sounded well trained. "But are you sure that your father approves of the deed?"

"Do you dare to doubt my word?" demanded Ujinobu. "Of course he approves of the deed!"

"Then why didn't he say something about this when I saw him earlier today?" asked the other man.

"This a momentous decision that he is making," said Ujinobu smoothly. "He wanted me to sound you out first. Don't worry. You will hear from him tomorrow morning."

In his effort to concentrate on the conversation, Matsuzo forgot to continue his soft snores. The stranger suddenly cried, "Are you sure the young ronin is asleep?"

Fighting down panic, Matsuzo forced himself to breathe in and out regularly. Finally he heard Ujinobu say, "He is asleep. I know that he and Bunkei between them finished all the sake, because I saw the empty jug. You're too nervous. Are you sure you are able to do it?"

"I think so," said the stranger. Even Matsuzo could hear the doubt in his voice, however.

"If you don't want to, we can get someone else in your company to take your place," said Ujinobu. "With the mask, nobody will know the difference."

"That won't be necessary," said the other man quickly. "I can do it, if it is Lord Ohmori's wish."

"All right, tomorrow morning my father will see you and give his official word," said Ujinobu. After a moment he added, "Those two ronin may become a nuisance. We may have to do something about them."

His voice was receding as he spoke, and soon there was total silence.

Zenta lowered his bamboo practice stick, stepped back, and stared at the red-faced, panting boy. Torazo had said that he was clumsy, and so had his mother. But Zenta was still unprepared for the boy's extraordinary ineptitude. His attacks had been badly timed and worse executed. Everything he did was disastrously wrong.

"Let's try that attack again," Zenta ordered. Snatching a sobbing breath, Torazo launched himself forward with desperate fury. Zenta knocked the stick flying from the boy's hands. Torazo fell to his knees, and as Zenta looked down at the small, shaking figure, he felt deeply puzzled.

"What is the name of your teacher?" he asked.

"Itoh Kenzaburo," mumbled Torazo, without raising his head.

It was a name that Zenta knew well. Kenzaburo was one of the three best swordsmen in western Japan, and Zenta had hoped to meet the man someday. "Why do you keep following the movement of your stick with your eyes?" he asked.

Slowly Torazo looked up. "Aren't you supposed to?"

"You should never do that!" said Zenta sharply. "I'm amazed that Kenzaburo would let you go on like this!"

"I see," said Torazo quietly. He picked up his stick and looked at it thoughtfully.

"The way you move your shoulders when you start your swing is also wrong..." began Zenta. He broke off when a sudden suspicion came to him. "When was the last time you had a lesson with Kenzaburo?"

Torazo swallowed. "About two months ago."

That explained a great deal, Zenta thought. He guessed that Torazo had probably rebelled against his teacher. Kenzaburo, unwilling to put up with the tantrums of his student, even a student of high rank, had probably left in disgust.

"Does that mean you've been practicing on your own for the last two months?" demanded Zenta.

When the boy was dumb, Zenta took his silence for assent. As Lord Kawai's son, Torazo had to master the sword. He was mature for his age and doubtless knew that his position was precarious. Even if he were unaware of his fathers plans for a second marriage, he must realize that he lived in a treacherous age when vassals often betrayed their lords. Being Lord Kawai's oldest son was no guarantee of a secure future. He had to win the loyalty of the Kawai men. Physically unattractive, with a moody personality to match, Torazo could command respect only by sheer ability. This was the age of the samurai, and the samurai's sword was his soul. For Torazo, swordsmanship was more than a useful skill: he needed it to survive.

This was a possible explanation of Torazo's solitary walks. Zenta guessed that when the farmer caught him in the field, Torazo was simply looking for a private place to practice swordsmanship away from the contemptuous eyes of his father's vassals. Again Zenta felt a wave of pity for the boy. He remembered his own youth and the teacher who had saved his life when he had been ready to kill himself out of despair and loneliness. The act of saving Torazo would be Zenta's offering to the memory of his dead teacher. Besides, he was beginning to have a great admiration for the boy's courage and determination.

"Don't practice by yourself from now on," Zenta told Torazo. "At your stage of development you can acquire bad habits that would take hard work to erase. In fact, that's what we must do right now: get rid of your bad habits."

Torazo stood up and gripped his stick. "All right."

An hour later, Zenta had to put a stop to the session. Torazo was trying too hard, and in his exhausted state he was almost deaf to instruction. "That's enough for today," Zenta said, trying to sound encouraging. "You've worked very hard, and you're tired. Let's practice again tomorrow."

Torazo could barely stand upright, but his eyes missed nothing. "It's no use, is it? I'm too clumsy!"

For an instant Zenta felt actual dislike for Lady Sayo, who had probably told Torazo repeatedly that he was hopelessly clumsy. Perhaps Lord Kawai and the fencing teacher, Kenzaburo, had also dwelt on the boy's clumsiness. "No one is naturally clumsy," Zenta said, and he was sincere. "You merely lack self-control: you rush into things without thought. But you have the build of a potential swordsman, and you're very strong."

"I'm too short," said Torazo bitterly.

72

Zenta laughed. "You'll grow. Of course you're small for your age, but you may have a sudden spurt of growth and catch up with the other boys. I wouldn't be surprised if you became a rather tall man. You have big hands and feet."

Torazo looked at his big-boned hands almost in wonder. He nodded.

"Why don't we meet at this place again tomorrow?" asked Zenta as cheerfully as he could.

The boy did not return Zenta's smile. "All right. I'll be back."

"By the way," said Zenta, "it's not a good idea for you to go about alone. In fact, I don't advise you to come to the inn at all, especially at night. Too many things can happen to you."

Torazo made no reply to this. He nodded and walked away without saying another word. Looking at the retreating figure, Zenta thought about the disturbing expression he had seen on the boy's face. When the corners of Torazo's lips twisted in that brief grimace, he looked exactly like Lord Kawai.

8

"I'm not going out tonight," vowed Matsuzo. "After last night's experience, I'm staying indoors no matter what happens." He tenderly fingered his scraped shin. The ugly scabs were a visible reminder that he should tend to his own business.

"What if they stage a Noh play under the cherry trees?" asked Bunkei.

Matsuzo, about to pick up a piece of fish, froze with chopsticks in hand. But it was Zenta who said, "From what Matsuzo told us, they won't do anything until they get Lord Ohmori's official word tomorrow morning."

After Matsuzo had told Zenta about the conversation he had overheard, they both felt that they should talk over the matter with Bunkei. The artist was familiar with local intrigues, and he had sharp wits, even if he was too lazy to move.

The three men had gone over the snatches of conversation thoroughly, and it was Bunkei who had declared that the man speaking to Ujinobu was most likely a Noh actor. The mention of the mask suggested that, because the leading actors of a Noh drama always wore masks. But by supper time they still couldn't agree on what it was the man was supposed to do. In the end they had decided to adopt an attitude of noninterference and wait.

Bunkei reached over for Matsuzo's rice bowl and refilled it. "The cherry tree vandal would be mad to try anything tonight," he said.

"After the fuss last night, he must know that Lord Ohmori has posted guards all over the place."

"But don't you think that the vandal is insane, anyway?" said Matsuzo. "We can't predict what a madman will do."

He glanced over at Zenta. It occurred to him that his friend was unusually tense this evening. He had finished eating before the others, and now he sat as if waiting for something. Finally Zenta broke his silence. "It's not raining tonight, and the moon is out. If the vandal comes, his capture is almost certain."

It was true. The moon was three-quarters full, and in its cold light the white boughs of the cherry trees looked faintly luminous. Anyone moving among the trees in the clearing would be highly visible.

"I don't think we'll have any trouble tonight," said Bunkei. He put down his chopsticks, sighed wistfully, and cocked a reproachful eye at Matsuzo. "You shouldn't have encouraged me to drink so much sake this afternoon. It would have been very nice to have some wine left for tonight."

Matsuzo was indignant. Bunkei had needed no encouragement that afternoon, and he was about to point this out when he suddenly heard shouts. Unexpectedly, the noise came not from the clearing but from the other side of the inn.

"The cunning devil!" said Zenta. "Everybody is expecting him to attack another tree in the clearing. Now it seems he must be after one of the trees outside the kitchen!"

The shouts grew louder, and soon they heard a rush of many feet. After a while the noise died down. Peering outside, Bunkei said, "They've lost him. You know, I can almost admire the man. To be able to outwit these men night after night…"

"I'm tempted to go out and have a look," said Matsuzo.

"Don't!" said Zenta. "Have you forgotten already that you're determined to stay out of trouble?"

But the choice to stay aloof was not theirs to make. They heard the sound of feet marching purposefully toward the tea house, and in the next instant the front door slid open with a crash. Samurai holding drawn swords crowded into the small house.

"I'm sorry, but we have orders from Lord Ohmori to search your house," said the leader. The apology was perfunctory, and he did not wait for a reply. His men spread out and began to look into every shelf and corner.

"If you tell us what you are looking for, perhaps we can help," Zenta offered courteously.

"We've had another cherry tree incident," explained the leader. He clenched his fist in frustration. "We were so close to catching him! He didn't even have time to finish the job this time. The branch was not completely broken off, and we even found the ax he used. He must still be around somewhere."

"You won't find him in my paintbrush holder," said Bunkei. "And be careful of that ink stick! It's valuable."

Suddenly they heard a woman's shriek coming from the direction of the inn. It was followed by some raucous male laughing. Then the woman's voice broke into a torrent of angry scolding.

"That sounds like Haru!" said Zenta, starting up. "Your men must be trying to molest her!"

Matsuzo was up as well. "I'll come with you!"

"Where do you think you're going?" demanded the leader.

Zenta's hand was on the hilt of his sword, and for a moment the air was heavy with danger. Then Bunkei said, "Wait. I think it's nothing serious."

He was right. Haru's voice was speaking more calmly, and it even ended with some laughter.

"The searchers must have burst into the girl's room at an embarrassing moment," said Bunkei. The two ronin put down their swords and subsided.

"Our men are not complete louts," said the leader testily. "Of course we try to use as much tact as possible."

"I'm sorry," said Zenta. He relaxed and smiled. "It's just that the last time I heard Haru shriek like that, she really was being attacked by soldiers."

Now that the tense moment had passed, the leader seemed more friendly. "I suppose the women were startled when our men burst in so unceremoniously. Lord Ohmori is determined to catch the vandal this time, and he gave orders to surround the whole area and let no one through while we search every corner for the fugitive."

Matsuzo actually came close to feeling sorry for the vandal. He remembered Lord Ohmori's anger on the previous night, and he knew that if the vandal were caught, he could expect little mercy. And it looked as if the man would certainly not escape the tight net around him.

The search of the tea house was soon completed, and the leader, after making a brief apology, rushed off with his men. Looking at the departing Ohmori samurai, Zenta said, "The search won't accomplish anything if the fugitive is someone staying at the inn. At this very moment he could be pretending to be one of the searchers."

"The innkeeper and his people would be the last to damage the cherry trees," objected Bunkei. "After all, the trees provide this valley with its greatest claim to fame."

"It could be one of the Ohmori men," said Matsuzo. "Perhaps he hates his master, and knowing how much Lord Ohmori loves cherry trees, chooses this way of hurting him." But he spoke idly and didn't really believe his own suggestion.

"Don't forget the mysterious Gonzaemon," said Zenta. "I really did see him running away last night. The trouble is, I can't think of any reason why he should do it."

"Last night Lord Ohmori was so ready to believe that we were the guilty ones," complained Matsuzo. "Why don't they drag Gonzaemon before Lord Ohmori and ask him a few questions?"

Bunkei's lips curled. "Because the innkeeper's wife is infatuated with him and will tell them that her beloved cousin was with her all evening."

Zenta opened one of the sliding panels and stepped out on the veranda. After a few moments, he returned, shaking his head. "They don't seem to be having much success with their search. Things are quieting down."

Incredibly, the vandal had escaped again. Although he could not condone the vandalism, Matsuzo began to share Bunkei's admiration for the man. He had to be wonderfully clever to escape the eyes of all these men who were waiting for him to strike. Unless Zenta's theory was right, that the man was someone staying at the inn or had an accomplice there.

Except for the sound of men passing in front of their house a few times, they could hear little activity. The Ohmori men seemed to be giving up the search. Matsuzo stretched and yawned. During the past few days he had done little but eat and sleep. As his glance fell on Bunkei's plump figure, he felt a twinge of alarm. Would he soon look like that if he continued his life of ease? Recalling that Zenta was to give lessons to Torazo the next day, Matsuzo decided that he would also embark on a program to get back into shape. But that was for tomorrow. Tonight he would go to bed early.

Just as he was about to stand up, he heard a faint scratching on the front door. Haru's voice said, "May I come in?"

"Yes, come in!" said Bunkei eagerly. "Tell us what happened at the inn tonight."

The door slid open, and Haru entered, carrying a tray with half a dozen small bottles of heated sake. At this sight Bunkei beamed. "Good girl! How you managed to think of wine..."

His voice trailed off as Haru turned to Zenta and whispered, "Please, sir, can you come with me to the inn? There is something I have to show you."

On the way to the inn, Zenta and Haru were challenged twice by guards but were allowed to proceed when they were recognized. Zenta knew that if they had been going away from the inn instead of toward it they would have received a more rigorous examination.

Haru was leading Zenta around the back of the inn, toward the house used by the innkeeper and his staff. She was going to show him the newly damaged tree behind the kitchen garden, thought Zenta. As they turned a corner, they saw Lord Ohmori standing with Ujinobu.

In the light of the lantern held by a maid, Lord Ohmori's face looked white and set. "I will see that Noh actor tomorrow morning and tell him my decision," he told his son. His voice was thick, the words barely intelligible. Clearly he was in the grip of a strong emotion. He pushed blindly past the ronin.

Ujinobu turned to follow his father. His smiling face was a complete contrast to Lord Ohmori's. Although the Ohmori men had apparently failed to capture the vandal, Ujinobu looked extremely pleased with himself. His smile faded when he saw Zenta and Haru. "What are you doing here?" he asked the ronin.

"I heard about the new outrage," said Zenta, "and I came to look at the damaged tree."

Something like triumph showed on Ujinobu's face. "All you will see is that the blow was struck from below again. And that proves, as you so cleverly said, that the vandal was someone short."

"I heard that you found an ax at the scene," said Zenta.

"Yes, we did. Would you like to see it?" Ujinobu continued to smile. "There it is on that stone. We haven't done anything to it. With your brilliance, perhaps you can deduce something."

Zenta bowed. "Thank you." Taking Haru's lantern, he went over to the stone and looked down at the ax. It seemed to be a perfectly ordinary ax. The blade was shining, and there was no stain or smudge on the handle.

"Well? Does the ax tell you anything?" asked Ujinobu.

"I don't know yet," admitted Zenta.

"Don't try to be too clever," sneered Ujinobu, turning away and stalking off.

Zenta started for the kitchen garden, but Haru whispered, "Not that way. Over here."

To his surprise, the girl led him to the bathhouse used by the staff of the inn and the innkeeper's family. It was a small hut detached from the rest of the house, and it contained a large, deep square tub made of cypress. Both Zenta and Matsuzo had bathed there earlier in the evening, before they ate dinner.

Haru glanced around carefully and entered the hut. After Zenta followed her inside, the girl closed the door, put down the lantern, and lifted the pieces of wooden boards that served as a lid for the tub. Sitting inside, with only his head and shoulders above water, was Torazo.

When Zenta recovered his tongue, the only thing he could think of saying to the boy was, "How did the searchers miss you?"

Haru giggled. "I made him get into the tub, and then I undressed and got into the tub, too. He was behind me, so the searchers couldn't see him."

Zenta could picture the scene: the searchers bursting into the hut and being confronted with the sight of the naked girl sitting in the bathtub. "So that was what all the shrieking and shouting was about," he said. "We heard you, and for a moment we thought the soldiers were attacking you."

"I had to put on a good show," explained Haru. "I scolded them so hard that they retreated without searching the room thoroughly."

It wasn't the scolding alone that had distracted the searchers, thought Zenta. People were used to public nakedness, since they bathed together in communal hotsprings and baths. Nonetheless, the sight of Haru's pearly shoulders had probably been enough to distract the minds of the searchers from their duty. It was interesting that the girl appeared quite unembarrassed. In some ways Haru was still like a child.

But what surprised Zenta was the glint in Torazo's eye as he slowly climbed out of the tub. Whereas Haru was innocent for her age, Torazo was unusually mature. I hope he doesn't turn out to be lecherous like his father, thought Zenta.

"What are you doing here at the inn?" he asked Torazo. "Didn't I tell you not to come tonight?"

The boy's face, which had been alive with amusement became secretive. "I had some unfinished business here."

"Your business can't be so important that it's worth the risk," said Zenta. "If you were caught, things could have been highly embarrassing. You know that, don't you?"

Torazo looked stubborn. "I know. You don't have to remind me."

"Can't you tell me the truth?" asked Zenta earnestly. Without speaking, the boy looked away and shook his head.

Zenta stared at him. He realized that he was making the mistake of expecting Torazo to behave the way he himself would have done at the age of fourteen. Torazo was a totally different person. He sighed and said, "I told you before that I will not help you if you are planning something dishonorable. Do you remember?"

"I do," muttered Torazo. "I'm planning nothing dishonorable." He began to shiver.

"He's getting cold!" said Haru. "I'll go and get him some dry clothes." She went off noiselessly.

Zenta gave a start as he saw some brown smears on the rim of the bathtub. "Are you wounded?"

Torazo followed his glance. "That's just soy sauce. When I first saw Haru tonight, she gave me some broiled rice cakes covered with soy sauce and syrup, and I got it all over my hands."

"I see," said Zenta slowly. The soy sauce smears gave him the answer to one of his questions, at least. He came to a decision. "Tell me what happened after you ate the rice cakes," he said to the boy.

"I...I finished what I came to do," said Torazo. His teeth were chattering slightly. "After that I got worried about how to get out again, so I went to Haru to see if she could help me. Then the shouting started. Haru hid me in the bathtub, and after the men left the bathhouse, I asked her to find you."

Soft steps approached the bathhouse, but it was only Haru returning with dry clothes. "Here, put these on," she whispered.

Torazo held up the kimono, and at the sight of the gaily patterned cloth, his voice cracked. "This is a girl's kimono!"

Zenta nearly laughed aloud. He saw that Haru was hoping to smuggle Torazo past the guards by disguising him as a girl. "Put it on," he told the boy. "After all, many heroes in our history have had to disguise themselves as girls. Why shouldn't you?"

After Torazo had stripped off his wet clothes and put on the dry kimono, Haru looked at him doubtfully. "Hm...we'll have to do something about his face."

"I know," said Torazo bitterly. "I'm too ugly."

The boy was no beauty, but he would not have been so conscious of his ugliness if someone — probably his mother — had not commented on it so often. "What does it matter?" Zenta said impatiently. "We can't all be as pretty as Ujinobu."

Haru giggled, and after a moment even Torazo smiled. "All right, let's not waste any more time," Zenta said briskly. "We'll have to distract the attention of the Ohmori men somehow, so that they won't look too closely at us when we dash past."

"Maybe I can get into conversation with some of the guards," suggested Haru.

"No!" said Zenta. "You've been too prominent already. I don't want Lord Ohmori getting suspicious of you. Besides, the men saw me enter the inn with you, and they will be suspicious if they see me leaving with a different girl."

Torazo hitched up his kimono until it was the right length and tried to tie it in place with the sash. "There is no way that you can make me look like Haru," he muttered angrily.

"Here, let me tie the sash for you," said Haru. When she finished, she surveyed her handiwork uneasily. "If they don't shine a light on you, it might be all right."

"I'll use my old trick to distract them," said Zenta.

"What trick is that?" asked Torazo.

"You'll see," said Zenta. "Come on."

They put out their lantern and opened the door of the bathhouse quietly. Outside, the moon was low, and by its light they could see their way, but it was not possible to distinguish faces.

"Take smaller steps," Haru told Torazo. "Girls don't stride like that."

It was quiet in the grounds of the inn, but they knew that the Ohmori guards were still alert for anything unusual. Zenta stooped and picked up a rock.

"Are you going to knock out one of the guards with that?" asked Torazo.

"Don't be so bloodthirsty," said Zenta. "Besides, knocking out a guard won't do any good. There are plenty of others."

As they approached the gate of the inn, Zenta said, "Haru and I will talk in a normal voice, so that the guards know we're coming. Say something to me, Haru."

"Yes, all right," said Haru. In a carrying voice, she said, "And we think that the tree can be saved this time. The vandal did not have time to cut all the way through the branch."

"Who is there?" shouted one of the guards.

"I came here earlier," replied Zenta. "Lord Ujinobu knows that I'm here."

The guard gave a grunt of recognition as Zenta and Haru passed in front of him, and then lost interest. After they walked to the storeroom near the entrance and were screened from the view of the guards, Zenta took out his rock. "You stay behind, Haru," he said quietly. "Your role tonight is finished." Then he threw the rock over the wall as hard as he could.

When they heard the rustle of its fall in the distance, he shouted, "What was that? I heard someone moving outside!"

"I heard him, too!" shouted one of the guards. He pushed open the gate and rushed out.

"There he is!" yelled Zenta, pointing outside.

Lanterns in hand, the other guards poured out after the first man, leaving the gate unlighted except for the moon.

"Let's go," Zenta told Torazo. They sprinted out in their turn.

When the sounds of the Ohmori men grew faint, Zenta slowed down and finally stopped. Torazo seemed to be having trouble catching his breath. But looking at him more closely, Zenta saw that the boy was laughing. Eventually Torazo got his breath under control. "I wonder if those men ever found the piece of rock you threw," he gasped.

Zenta regarded the boy soberly. "You are enjoying yourself. That would be fine if you were a ronin with no ties and no responsibilities. But don't forget that for someone in your position, an amusing adventure can lead to disaster." This was the first time Zenta alluded to the fact that Torazo was the son of Lord Kawai. Because of Torazo's close escape, it was no longer possible to ignore it.

"Perhaps you didn't appreciate how serious the consequences could be if you had been caught by the Ohmori men tonight," continued Zenta. "They would suspect you of having vandalized the cherry trees. Since you are the son of Lord Kawai, they wouldn't dare harm you physically, but this could cause a serious breach between your father and Lord Ohmori."

Torazo became equally sober. "I understand. You don't have to say any more." As they walked toward Sairyuji Temple, he glanced at Zenta out of the corner of his eye. "But I still want to continue my lessons with you."

"There is no reason why you shouldn't," said Zenta, hoping that his slight hesitation in answering was not noticeable. "But don't come near the inn again. It's too risky. Why don't we meet again at the place where we practiced this afternoon?"

"All right," said Torazo. "I'll come to the clearing again."

Zenta noticed that although Torazo had agreed to have his lessons in the clearing, he had not promised to avoid the inn entirely. But it was obviously impossible to persuade the boy to reveal his reasons for visiting the inn. As Zenta watched Torazo pass through the gate of Sairyuji Temple, he wondered if he had made a mistake in becoming involved with the affairs of the Kawai family. So far it was mainly pity that caused him to help the moody, secretive boy — and pity alone could not fashion a good swordsman out of unpromising material.

Ujinobu was sitting in his room drinking sake when one of his men reported to him. "I'm sorry, my lord, but we could find no trace of the vandals."

After the man left, Ujinobu turned to his companion and smiled. "It doesn't matter. My father caught a glimpse of him just before he ran away."

9
九

The two ronin agreed that the plot Matsuzo had overheard would have to be investigated. Since a Noh actor seemed to be involved, they decided that they should try to smuggle themselves into the audience for the performance. The person who could help them was the abbot of Sairyuji Temple, and after breakfast the two men wasted no time in climbing the hill to the temple.

There was still local mist in the valley. When Matsuzo looked back, the scene was like a landscape painting in which the artist had dipped a wide brush in water and brought it back and forth across the paper, leaving swaths of blankness. The rest of the picture showed cherry trees delicately printed by the fine point of the brush.

"It's so beautiful," murmured Matsuzo. "How could anyone scheme and plot, when he could be enjoying the cherry blossoms?"

Zenta grinned. "As the abbot said, any violence committed in the midst of such beauty would be a lapse of good taste."

"I thought the abbot sounded a little unfeeling, for such a holy man," said Matsuzo.

Zenta shook his head. "The abbot was not unfeeling, merely wise. He knew perfectly well that an appeal to compassion in men like Lord Kawai or Lord Ohmori would be useless. But many warlords wish to be considered men of refinement and copy the manners of the courtiers in the capital. The abbot therefore appealed not to their compassion but to their snobbishness."

"Well, I hope Lord Ohmori's snobbishness will prevent bloodshed during a Noh play," said Matsuzo.

"Don't depend on it," warned Zenta. "Remember — he was quite ready to behead us under the very cherry trees he admired so much."

"I wish I knew exactly what Ujinobu was asking that actor to do," said Matsuzo. "We'll find out during the performance this afternoon, I suppose."

As it turned out, they were to discover Ujinobu's intentions much sooner. When they sent in their names at the gate of Sairyuji Temple and asked to see the abbot, a young monk told them that the abbot was with a visitor, and would be unable to see them.

It was a disappointment. "Maybe Lady Sayo could do something," said Matsuzo finally. He remembered her searching eyes on Zenta. "After the way you helped Torazo last night, the least she can do is have someone find us two places for this afternoon's performance."

"My guess is that Torazo told his mother nothing at all about his adventures last night," said Zenta. "You know, I'd rather not ask Lady Sayo's help if we can avoid it. She makes me nervous."

Matsuzo nearly laughed aloud. He was glad to discover that he was not the only one intimidated by Lady Sayo. "I know what you mean," he said. "She makes me feel as if my sash is untied and my loincloth is showing."

"Let's come back later, when the abbot isn't busy," suggested Zenta.

Matsuzo agreed. It was time to leave, for the guards at the gate were beginning to look at them suspiciously. Just as they turned away, however, the young monk came running back. "Wait!" he cried. "Don't go! The abbot wants to see you!"

The abbot's visitor was still there when the two ronin were shown into his small study. The visitor was a man just entering middle age, but he was still dressed with the patterned kimono and striped sash of a fashionable young man. His carriage was graceful and the pose of his hands beautiful in spite of his agitation. There was no mistaking his agitation. Matsuzo could see it in the man's wide, panic filled-eyes and his trembling lips.

The abbot looked gravely at the two ronin as they bowed to him. "I think you had better hear this man's story. He is the leading actor in the Noh company engaged by Lord Ohmori to give a performance this afternoon."

Matsuzo started. "You must be the man I heard talking to Ujinobu yesterday!"

"What?" cried the actor. "How did you hear?" His voice threatened to rise, and the abbot put his hand on the actors shoulder to calm him.

"I was inside the tea house when you and Ujinobu were having your discussion," explained Matsuzo. "But I didn't hear what you were planning to do. You kept talking about getting orders directly from Lord Ohmori."

The actor caught his breath in a sob. "Yes, I see what happened now. You're one of the young ronin staying with the artist Bunkei. Ujinobu told me you had drunk a great deal of sake and were fast asleep."

"Well, I wasn't," said Matsuzo. "My head isn't as weak as all that."

He was interrupted by the abbot. "Tell them what Ujinobu's plan was," he said to the actor.

Even when desperate, the actor could not refrain from drama. "Ujinobu told me to assassinate Lord Kawai," he said simply. Then he folded his hands, bowed his head, and held the graceful pose completely unmoving for the space of ten seconds, a feat possible only after hard training.

Zenta broke the long silence. "According to Matsuzo here, you refused to undertake the task unless you heard the order from Lord Ohmori himself. Did you?"

The actor nodded. "Lord Ohmori personally gave the order for the assassination."

Matsuzo remembered the actor's voice urgently begging to hear the order directly from Lord Ohmori, and Ujinobu's telling him to wait until the next morning. It would appear that at the time of the conversation Lord Ohmori had not decided on the assassination.

Apparently Zenta felt the same, for he said to the actor, "At first you thought, didn't you, that the assassination was not really Lord Ohmori's idea?"

"Yes, that's what I thought," said the actor. "I suspected that Ujinobu was lying when he claimed the order came from his father. But my doubts were settled this morning when I was summoned into

Lord Ohmori's presence. I heard the order for the assassination from his own lips."

"That means Lord Ohmori was still undecided yesterday afternoon, but something happened in the course of the evening to make up his mind!" exclaimed Zenta. "I actually overheard him tell Ujinobu last night that he was going to announce his decision to a Noh actor!"

Matsuzo was still suspicious. "You've got what you wanted, namely Lord Ohmori's personal command," he said to the actor. "Then why are you betraying the plot to us?"

The actor dropped his eyes, and it was Zenta who answered for him. "He is afraid that as soon as he kills Lord Kawai he will be cut down by the Kawai men and Lord Ohmori won't lift a finger to help him."

Matsuzo began to understand. "I see — it would be very convenient for Lord Ohmori if the assassin were silenced on the spot."

The abbot turned to Zenta. "What can we do to prevent this disaster? Can we warn Lord Kawai somehow?"

"I've been trying all morning to smuggle a message to Lord Kawai," said the actor. His desperation was pitiable. "But there is always somebody from the Ohmori family with him. I'm certain that between now and the Noh performance he will be closely watched."

The abbot nodded thoughtfully. "That is true. Lord Kawai brought only a small retinue with him, and the Ohmori samurai are everywhere. It will be very difficult to send a message to him without alerting the Ohmori men."

"So," murmured Zenta. "By his infatuation with Lady Ayame, Lord Kawai has allowed himself and his family to fall into a deadly trap."

But Matsuzo was still not completely convinced of the actor's story. "Why doesn't Lord Ohmori simply order his men to kill Lord Kawai and his party? Why does he have to resort to theatricals?"

"I think I can answer that," said Zenta. "Lord Ohmori probably hopes to win over some of Lord Kawai's other vassals as well. They wouldn't support him if they knew he murdered his master. That's why it's best if the murder were committed by someone not connected with the Ohmori clan."

That sounded likely, thought Matsuzo. He finally understood the efforts of the Ohmori family to enlist Zenta and himself into their service. "They tried at first to recruit *us* as Lord Kawai's assassins, didn't they?"

Zenta nodded. "But we were not very cooperative. In any case, an actor is easier to kill afterwards, whereas there is a small chance that we might succeed in escaping and revealing the true story."

The actor moaned. "I'm lost. They'll kill me if I refuse to assassinate Lord Kawai, and they'll kill me if I *do* assassinate him."

Looking at the frightened actor, Matsuzo had to agree that the man presented a much easier disposal problem. The only thing Ujinobu had not counted on was that the actor would realize he was marked for death and run to the abbot for help.

"The situation is serious," said the abbot. "Even if we manage to warn Lord Kawai, he and his party would never be permitted to leave this valley alive. Lord Ohmori couldn't afford to let him escape."

"We can at least try to bring Torazo and Lady Sayo to safety," said Zenta.

"What about me?" cried the actor. "What about the assassination?"

"You must think of a way to stop the assassination," the abbot told Zenta.

Matsuzo began to resent the abbot's attitude. Why should he and Zenta risk their lives to save someone they didn't like, someone who had even ordered them to be killed? "We'll do what we can to save Lady Sayo and the boy, but..." he began.

"Assassination is wicked, and knowing that it is planned, you cannot shut your eyes," said the abbot.

The words put Matsuzo to shame. The abbot was right. They had to prevent the assassination, not so much for the sake of Lord Kawai as for the sake of their own honor.

"I'll do my best, but I'm not optimistic," said Zenta. The abbot nodded gravely. "Your best will satisfy me."

Zenta turned to the actor. "Tell me how you are supposed to carry out the assassination. Surely you don't expect to get off the stage, march up to Lord Kawai, and plunge a dagger into his breast?"

The actor summoned a feeble smile and shook his head. "Lord Kawai is an enthusiastic amateur performer of Noh, and he can chant many of the famous passages by heart. We offered to let him play the leading role for one of the scenes. I will play the secondary role, and

I am to attack him when we two are alone on the stage. Nobody else will be close enough to interfere."

"Perhaps I can disguise myself as a stagehand," mused Zenta. "They are always going on and off the stage while the play is in progress to put on or remove props. I can even hand Lord Kawai a message of warning in full view of the audience and pretend it's one of the stage props. Nobody ever looks at a stagehand."

When the actor mentioned amateur performances of Noh, an idea began to grow in Matsuzo's mind. The more he thought about it, the more promising it seemed. Furthermore, it would satisfy a secret ambition of his. "Can you tell me," he asked the actor, "in which play you are planning to appear with Lord Kawai?"

"The play is *Cherry Viewing at Yoshino*," replied the actor. "We chose it because of its appropriateness to the season. Why do you want to know?"

It was a play that Matsuzo knew very well. He beamed happily. "This is my idea: I will take your place, and while I'm on the stage with Lord Kawai I'll whisper a warning. Since I'll be wearing a mask, nobody will know the difference."

Matsuzo expected the actor to be overjoyed by this solution to his difficulties. Instead, the actor looked affronted. "But you are not trained! Everyone will think that I'm giving a terrible performance!"

Matsuzo was stung by the insult. "I know the lines, and I won't disgrace you! Do you want your life saved, or don't you?"

"All right but I'll have to coach you carefully on the gestures and the voice projection," muttered the actor, who seemed to be worried more by the possible damage to his reputation than by the danger to his life.

"But will this save Lord Kawai?" the abbot asked Matsuzo. "When the Ohmori men see that you are not acting according to plan, they might rush on stage and attack both of you."

"I can arrange a distraction in another part of the courtyard," suggested Zenta. "While I engage the attention of the Ohmori samurai, Matsuzo and Lord Kawai can fight their way out."

"Some of my monks can help you do that," said the abbot.

Zenta's face suddenly darkened. "We must think of a way to rescue Torazo as well. He is in as much danger as Lord Kawai. Will he be attending the Noh performance?"

The abbot frowned and shook his head. "The boy left the temple this morning. Nobody has been able to discover where he has gone."

Zenta and Matsuzo stared at each other in consternation. Finally Zenta said, "He may be on his way to the inn. No, wait — we would have seen him then. He could have gone to the clearing where I gave him lessons yesterday."

"Do you think he is in any danger?" asked Matsuzo.

"I know he is in danger," said Zenta grimly.

"Then you must find the boy and save him," said the abbot.

"But Matsuzo needs help to escape with Lord Kawai," protested Zenta. "They can't break out of here alone!"

"My monks and I will think of some way to help them escape," the abbot told Zenta. "It is your job to save the boy."

"Don't worry about us," Matsuzo said. "The Ohmori men are expecting an actor not a warrior. We'll take them completely by surprise."

Zenta nodded assent. Torazo had no hope at all of surviving without help, whereas Lord Kawai and Matsuzo assisted by the abbot and monks of Sairyuji Temple might have a chance of escaping. Although Sairyuji did not belong to one of the more warlike sects, Zenta knew that a couple of the monks there had been samurai in an earlier life. They would probably relish the prospect of some action again. After discussing various schemes with the abbot on how to distract the attention of the Ohmori men, Zenta slipped quietly out the door.

The Noh drama had always been patronized by samurai audiences. The bare austerity of the stage, the minimal use of props and the resigned, understated movements of the actors all appealed to a warrior class that placed a high value on self-control. Many famous warlords were keen amateur performers. It was not surprising that even Lord Kawai, who showed little patience with poetry and music, was pleased to play a role in a famous Noh troupe.

Matsuzo had been taught to appreciate Noh at an early age, and with his interest in poetry and drama he had become an ardent fan. Rehearsing his role in the abbot's study, he was soon caught up by the excitement of playing on a real Noh stage, in full brilliant costume and before a distinguished audience. It was something he had always dreamed about. His voice throbbed with feeling and his gestures flowed freely as he went over his lines with the actor. The role was trivial compared to that of Lord Kawai, but he was determined to give it his best effort.

When he finished his speech, he looked to the actor for approval. To his surprise, the actor's face was screwed in a sour grimace. "No, no! You overdo your gestures! Why must you wave your arms like that? Amateurs always wave their arms too much!"

Matsuzo was crushed. "But..."

"If you have no reason to move, keep still," said the actor. Although he had been trembling for his life only a short while ago, he was now showing unexpected spirit.

"Don't worry so much," said the abbot soothingly. "Remember that Lord Kawai is an amateur, too. They will play very well together."

The actor wrung his hands. "The performance will be a travesty! My troupe will be the laughingstock of the country!"

"Well, if you'd rather play the role yourself..." began Matsuzo huffily.

"Please calm yourselves," begged the abbot. "You have very little time before the performance. Don't worry about the reaction of the audience. There will be so much confusion and even violence that nobody will remember the acting at all."

At the mention of violence, the actor's anger died and the look of fear was back in his eyes. "Very well," he muttered. He turned to Matsuzo. "We'll just work on making your performance at least plausible."

The mountain path was windy and treacherous with loose stones Nevertheless, Zenta almost ran toward the small clearing where he had given lessons to Torazo on the previous day. He was sure that the boy was there, and he was afraid that others were bent on reaching the clearing as well.

Zenta wondered about his own sense of urgency. Why was he so sure that Torazo's life was in danger? If the Ohmori insurrection succeeded, Torazo might be forced into a monastery to become a monk. With his unprepossessing looks and personality, he probably had little support among his father's vassals and would not be a threat. It should not be necessary to kill him. Lord Ohmori, except when aroused over the subject of cherry trees, seemed humane as warlords went. Moreover Lady Ayame would be sure to argue against murdering the boy.

Now, if Torazo had been caught lurking at the inn during the uproar over the cherry tree vandalism, the consequences would have been disastrous. But with Haru's help, Zenta had succeeded in smuggling Torazo out to safety. Then why did he still fear for the boy's life?

At a faint sound behind him, Zenta stopped and whirled around. His sword was out before he realized that the sound had been caused by pebbles falling into the ravine, dislodged by his feet, probably. He sheathed his sword and ran on, tying up his long sleeves with a thin cord as he went, to keep them out of the way in case of action. He expected action.

The interesting thing, thought Zenta, was that he felt more rather than less sympathy for Torazo after learning that he was Lord Kawai's son. Perhaps it was because he remembered Lady Sayo's cold and contemptuous look as she spoke of her son. Torazo's chances of succeeding his father also looked poor. If Lady Ayame married Lord Kawai and produced a son, it was quite possible that her son, with the powerful backing of the Ohmori family could seize the succession from Torazo.

In view of this, Lord Ohmori's decision to betray his feudal overlord was strange. Unconsciously Zenta slowed his steps as he puzzled over the problem. Lord Ohmori had much to gain if he stayed loyal to his master. Why, then, did he choose a course of action that was sure to bring him dishonor? Zenta didn't think that Lord Ohmori was at heart a treacherous man. His son, Ujinobu, looked capable of treachery, but was his influence over his father powerful enough? Zenta knew that in this cynical age of civil wars vassals had been known to betray their masters, but such betrayal was a violation of the samurai code and was undertaken only under a compelling reason. What was Lord Ohmori's reason?

But such speculations were useless, since Lord Ohmori had already made his decision. Zenta quickened his steps again. The clearing was just around the next corner, and as he turned the corner, he saw to his immense relief that Torazo was standing alone, practicing swings with a wooden stick.

Zenta was just about to call out a greeting when he was brought up short by a sight that drained the blood from his face. Armed men were pouring down the hillside across the clearing. If they surrounded Torazo, there would be no hope.

Zenta cupped his hands around his mouth and shouted, "Torazo! This way! Hurry!"

The boy threw a startled look at Zenta and another one at the men rushing down the hillside. He hesitated for two seconds — it seemed like an eternity — and then picked up his stick and ran toward Zenta.

"Those men look like Ohmori samurai," he said, as the two ran up the windy mountain path. "They are my father's vassals. Why are we running away from them?"

"Your father's ex-vassals," corrected Zenta. "If you're not convinced, look at their naked swords. That's hardly the way to greet the son of their feudal lord."

Zenta had to be blunt, because there was no time to be anything else. He hoped that Torazo would not be too crushed by the treachery of the Ohmori men.

Torazo seemed to take the news stoically. He ran in silence for a moment and then said, "What is happening to my father?"

It would be pointless to hide the truth. "There is a plot to kill him during the Noh play, but Matsuzo and the abbot of Sairyuji Temple have devised a plan to help him."

"What are his chances of escape?" asked Torazo. He was breathing hard and would soon be spent.

"About as good as ours," admitted Zenta.

"And my mother?"

Zenta felt a flash of guilt. He had forgotten to plan for Lady Sayo's escape. That was partly because she looked so cool and competent that one trusted her to protect herself. "I don't think Lord Ohmori sees any advantage in harming her," he said. "Perhaps the abbot can offer her a refuge. In any case, she is safer with him than with us."

The boy nodded and ran doggedly on. The path was now uphill and Torazo's steps were noticeably lagging. Zenta spared a brief glance backward and saw that their pursuers were gaining fast. Soon he would have to turn and make a stand.

They were badly outnumbered, and Torazo was more of a liability than a help. Zenta needed a place where the terrain could be used to his advantage. The mountain path was too narrow for more than one abreast — that was helpful, since the pursuers could only attack them one at a time. But the left edge of the path faced a sheer drop into a ravine whose bottom was obscured by trees. Torazo was already weaving with fatigue and Zenta's breath caught every time the boy stumbled near the edge.

To the right of the path the ground rose steeply. Zenta's aim was to make his stand at a place where the hill side of the path was a cliff too steep to afford a foothold. Then their pursuers would not be able to climb above and behind them.

But the choice of location was not his to make. Torazo's foot slipped on loose gravel, and he pitched forward on his face. As he struggled up, the first of their pursuers was upon them.

Zenta's sword was out as soon as he saw Torazo go down. He cut down the first man on an upward stroke and in the same continuous motion caught the second man with the return stroke. The third man was stronger: he parried Zenta's slash and tried for a remise. Zenta ducked under the attack, opened the way with a feint, and stabbed through the opening before the man could recover.

After that there was a respite as the rest of the pursuers drew back to consider their next step. Zenta made a rapid count. There seemed to be about twenty-five men. He had faced odds like this before, but in most cases his opponents had been rabble, badly trained ronin, or bandits. These Ohmori samurai were picked men. Nevertheless, he was confident that by conserving strength he could hold his own if they attacked him in ones and twos.

By some invisible agreement, a second wave of attackers ran forward. The leader went down immediately under Zenta's slash, but the second man tried to reach past to strike at Torazo. Zenta's left hand flashed out with his shorter sword and caught the man before he could strike the boy. The shorter sword was normally reserved for ceremonial use, but there were a few swordsmen who had mastered the technique of using both swords at once. The third man, seeing his comrades down, turned and ran.

The easy pickings appeared to be over thought Zenta, as he watched the rest of the pursuers retreat cautiously and whisper among themselves. He turned to Torazo and said, "Get behind me, and stay out of reach."

"No, I want to help you!" said Torazo.

"You will help me most by staying out of harm, so I don't have to worry about you!" snapped Zenta. He thought that it was fortunate the pursuers had not brought archers. But of course they had thought that Torazo was to be their only quarry.

The next group of attackers rushed up, less reckless than their predecessors, but curiously stubborn. Zenta felt slightly sick as he cut down men who were, after all, only obeying orders. But he had no choice. He had to kill or disable these men, not merely chase them back.

A scrabbling sound made him look up. He now understood the reason for the stubbornness of the last attack: they were keeping him busy while their comrades climbed the hillside above them. One of the men had picked up a big rock and was poised to throw it.

There was no time to shout a warning. Zenta threw himself at Torazo and felt the rock graze the back of his head. As he fell with Torazo, his body tensed to hit the ground, roll over and spring up in one practiced motion. But instead of hitting the ground, he encountered for one heart-stopping instant only space, empty space. The next few moments were a confused whirl of falling stones, tree branches, dank earth, and even flashes of blue sky. Mixed with the sharp, bright pain in his head was the hope that the cherry blossoms at the bottom of the ravine would cushion their fall.

10

十

Matsuzo had been concentrating so hard on rehearsing his lines, practicing his gestures, and adjusting his costume that time passed more quickly than he expected. He hadn't even noticed when the audience for the performance had assembled. And now he was waiting alone in the little costume room. The actor was on stage performing the first piece, a demon play ending in a spectacular dance. The voices of the chorus swooped, glided and rose into falsetto.

The part of the demon was an extremely taxing one, and peeking out between the curtains of the dressing room, Matsuzo had to admit that the role was far beyond his capabilities. The tempo of the dance increased to the beat of the hand drums and finally climaxed as the flutes shrilled out in frenzy. The dance ended with the actor racing off along the gangway, the wooden walk connecting the stage with the dressing room.

The actor burst into the dressing room and stood panting, still in his horned demon mask. Only after his breathing steadied did he slowly reach up to remove his mask. Underneath, his face showed some of the wildness of the demon role, but gradually his eyes lost their fixedness and his mouth its tautness. He closed his eyes and sighed. After a long moment he turned to Matsuzo. "Are you ready?"

The young ronin nodded and began to put on his mask. It was an old man's mask, with slitted eyes and a small white beard attached. Then, before he was quite ready, he heard the wooden sticks clapping together at an accelerating tempo, signaling his entrance. Swallowing hard, he parted the curtains leading to the gangway and made his entrance.

As he made his stately progress from the gangway to the stage, he wondered how he could whisper the warning to Lord Kawai. He had to convince the warlord quickly, because if the Ohmori men realized what he was doing they might surge on stage and cut both of them down before they had a chance to escape.

Perhaps he should begin with the words, "I'm supposed to assassinate you." But no, that was too risky. Lord Kawai might think that Matsuzo was the assassin announcing his intention, and he might yell for his men to defend him. That would be fatal. It was best to say, "There is a plot to assassinate you," and hope that Lord Kawai would follow directions.

Matsuzo suddenly realized that he was standing on the stage, facing the audience, about to deliver the opening lines of the play. There was just one problem: he couldn't remember which play it was. His mind was a total blank.

For a long, long moment he stood completely motionless. He sensed the musicians beginning to rustle uneasily behind him, and a tide of panic rose to engulf him.

Desperately, he tried to remember Zenta's words on achieving mental composure: if your mind is a blank, let the emptiness be your friend, not your enemy; use it as an interval for gathering your strength. He made himself breathe regularly, using his diaphragm, and soon he felt his racing heart slow down.

Of course. The play was *Cherry Viewing at Yoshino*, and the opening lines came to his lips without conscious effort. His voice was too high and tremulous, but it suited his role, which was that of an old priest. He realized to his relief that the audience probably thought his long silence had been a device to heighten the drama.

On the whole he was pleased with himself as he finished his opening lines. Why had the Noh actor worried so much? Amateurs could put on a very decent performance. The chorus and the musicians now took up the narrative, while Matsuzo retired to a corner of the stage and waited for the entrance of his fellow actor.

The drums beat faster, and the flutes joined in to pave the way for the entrance of the principal character. Lord Kawai had disdained the use of the actor's dressing room and had put on his costume in his own room. He now made his way down the gangway to the accompaniment of admiring murmurs from the audience. The admiration was for his costume, the brilliant trailing brocade robe of a court lady, shimmering with gold, vermilion, and pale green. On his face was the mask of a beautiful young girl. The mask was a masterpiece of woodcarving, capable of displaying various emotions depending on the light and the angle presented to the viewer. Now it showed serenity, now gaiety, and now a hint of wistfulness.

Lord Kawai's role was that of a beautiful girl who later revealed herself to the old priest as the spirit of the cherry trees. Looking on critically, Matsuzo thought that in spite of the beautiful robe and mask, Lord Kawai's performance was lacking in polish. Why did he have to wave his arms so much?

The opening lines of the young girl ended, and Matsuzo moved forward for his dialogue with Lord Kawai. This was the moment he had chosen for delivering his warning about the assassination. He took two gliding steps forward — and felt his mask slip down over his eyes.

He knew what had happened. In his haste before his entrance, he had not fastened the strings of the mask properly. The eye slits were narrow to begin with, and the tiny shift in position was enough to cut off his vision completely. He could not retie the strings right under the eyes of the audience of course. As he delivered the priest's greeting to the girl, he waved his arms expansively and ended with a flourish of his right hand pushing the mask upward.

It was a mistake. He merely loosened the string further and made the mask slip down a little more. The false beard of the mask was already tickling his chest, and at this rate he would soon be able to see over the top of the mask.

Lord Kawai's voice came, much closer than Matsuzo expected. He realized that he had to step back out of the way and be quick about it.

He pivoted and took one step back. In the next instant there was a rip, and Lord Kawai's voice whispered viciously in his ear, "You're stepping on my sleeve!"

Matsuzo jumped. Then he realized that this was his opportunity. "My lord," he said quickly, "there is a plot…"

He was not quick enough. Lord Kawai had moved off, and from the sound of his footsteps, there was now the length of the stage between them. Matsuzo discovered that the time had come to deliver his next lines.

Now, amateur Noh performers customarily memorize whole plays, instead of submerging themselves in a particular role. Matsuzo had not really identified himself with the role of the old priest. In his agitation, he skipped over the words of the priest and jumped ahead to the lines of the young girl.

Lord Kawai, another amateur performer, automatically responded with the lines of the old priest. The play lurched forward, with the two men unconsciously exchanging roles. Suddenly, Matsuzo came to a dead stop as he realized what was happening. Lord Kawai's voice also faltered to a stop. There was a total silence. This was finally broken by a titter from someone in the audience, which quickly changed to a cough.

"What's the matter with you?" hissed Lord Kawai. "Are you drunk?"

Matsuzo decided it was time to act. Clutching out blindly at Lord Kawai, he said quickly, "Lord Ohmori is planning to assassinate you!"

He felt Lord Kawai recoil — he probably thought Matsuzo was a drink-crazed actor — and he put his foot down hard on the warlord's trailing skirt. As Lord Kawai turned away, he tripped and fell, pulling Matsuzo down with him. There were several gasps from the audience. The masks of both men fell off, and Matsuzo rolled over until he faced the back of the stage. Pinning Lord Kawai down, he said under the noise of the audience, "I'm supposed to stab you with a knife. After I raise my hand and pretend to strike, will you lie still?"

Lord Kawai was neither stupid nor slow. His eyes widened at Matsuzo's words, but he gave a brief jerk of his head to signify that he understood.

With his back to the audience, Matsuzo raised his hand and pretended to strike down with his folded fan. Lord Kawai's body arched upward and gave a realistic convulsion. Then he fell back and lay still.

Cries of horror, genuine or otherwise, came from the audience. Above the noise, Matsuzo heard Lord Ohmori's voice, "Kill the assassin!"

At that point the intended victim nearly spoiled everything. Lord Kawai opened his eyes and raised himself on his elbows. "You're wrong about Ohmori!" he told Matsuzo. "Look! He's horrified by the assassination!"

It was then that the much needed distraction promised by the abbot finally came. A young monk rushed into the courtyard and cried, "We caught somebody vandalizing a cherry tree!"

Every head in the audience turned. Lord Ohmori started to his feet, forgetting even the assassination.

Matsuzo jumped up. "Come on," he said to Lord Kawai. "It's time to leave."

"Wait, I'm not sure that..." began Lord Kawai. Matsuzo's patience snapped. "I promised the abbot to help you, and I've done my best. If you don't want to follow, it doesn't matter in the least to me!"

The young ronin's indifference turned out to be more persuasive than any argument he could muster. Lord Kawai was a man of quick decision. He jumped to his feet and ran after Matsuzo up the gangway. The two men burst through the dressing room and sped across the covered walk to the back of the temple.

If Lord Kawai had any doubts left they were dispelled by the looks of the Ohmori samurai. On seeing their feudal overlord alive and well, their eyes showed consternation, not relief.

A small back gate had been left open for them by the abbot. As Matsuzo and Lord Kawai rushed through the gate and into the hills behind the temple, they could hear the sounds of fighting in the courtyard. The handful of Kawai men, seeing their master's danger, were trying to delay the Ohmori men and hold back pursuit. But they were badly outnumbered, and they wouldn't be able to keep up the resistance for long.

Lord Kawai turned to Matsuzo. "Shall we head north? That's the shortest way out of Ohmori territory."

"That's exactly what our pursuers will expect us to do," panted Matsuzo. He stopped for a moment to catch his breath. "So we'll go in the opposite direction. The abbot told a couple of his monks to run north. The Ohmori men will mistake them for us and spend valuable time chasing them."

Lord Kawai's expression showed that he did not think highly of the plan. "And what do we do? Run until we drop from exhaustion?"

"We'll go to the last place they expect," said Matsuzo. "We're going to the inn to meet Zenta and your son. After that, we'll think of something."

He was conscious first of the ache in his ribs. The sharp pain in the back of his head had spread through the whole of his skull. It throbbed, sending waves of nausea over him. He started to groan and discovered that something was covering his mouth.

Alarm jangled through his mind, and Zenta opened his eyes. The first thing he saw was Torazo's face looking down at him with desperate anxiety. He realized that it was Torazo's hand covering his mouth. The boy pointed upward and shook his head warningly, and then slowly withdrew his hand.

Zenta understood that Torazo was warning him to keep quiet. In a moment he knew why: there were voices coming from above.

"I think we should go down into the ravine and make sure of them."

"Don't be silly! How can they possibly survive the fall?"

"But they may not have struck bottom. What if their fall was checked by some tree branches?"

"I heard them fall all the way, I tell you. There's a stream at the bottom of the ravine, and there was an unmistakable splash."

A new voice joined in. "That's right. I heard the splash, too."

Zenta cautiously raised himself on his elbow and was immediately jolted by a stab of pain in the back of his head. Wincing, he looked around. The two of them were on a narrow ledge, too narrow to offer security by itself. What had saved them was a wild cherry tree growing out of the side of the mountain. They were wedged by the tree trunk, and the spreading blossom-covered branches shielded them from the view of the men above them. By the ache in his ribs, Zenta suspected that he had slammed into the tree on his way down the ravine, and judging from the voices of the men above, they couldn't have fallen very far.

Why did the men say that they had heard something strike the bottom of the ravine? Zenta suddenly remembered the rock which had grazed his head. It must have made the splash that the men had heard.

Meanwhile the Ohmori men were still talking.

"Come on, we're wasting time here. Those two must be dead."

"Yes, we'd better go. We have four men here badly hurt, and they need immediate attention."

"Shouldn't we at least leave a few men here to wait? There is a chance that the boy or the ronin may have survived the fall and will try to climb back up."

"No, we need all the men to carry the dead and the wounded."

Zenta heard some grunts and moans. Obviously the men were picking up their wounded comrades and getting ready to leave. Finally a voice said, "All right, we're going."

The sound of footsteps crunching on gravel grew fainter, until at last there was silence.

Torazo started to rise, but Zenta seized his wrist and held him back. He pointed above and motioned for silence. The announcement about going away had been made in a voice that seemed unnecessarily loud and distinct, and Zenta feared that it was a trick.

Torazo understood immediately. He swallowed and nodded. Looking at the boy's tear-streaked face, Zenta now knew it was more than pity that made him decide to help Torazo: it was also admiration for the boy's indomitable courage. He had stayed silent under the farmer's thrashing, and now, with his face badly scratched and one cheek scraped raw, he had the presence of mind to keep totally still.

Zenta wasn't sure how much time had passed. It seemed like an eternity, but it was probably only a few minutes. Finally, just as he thought that it was safe to move, he heard the voice:

"All right. Nothing moved. They must really be dead."

More footsteps sounded and receded into the distance. Zenta and Torazo silently looked at each other, and again they waited.

Zenta felt the pulse beat in his throat, each beat accompanied by a throb in his aching head. A wave of nausea rose in his chest and he knew that he was going to be sick very soon. Surely it was safe now to get up.

Torazo apparently felt the same. "They must be gone by now," he whispered.

"Yes, I think so," said Zenta. He sat up and was instantly sick. During the violent retching, he discovered that his ribs, though bruised, were not broken. At the end he wiped his mouth with his sleeve. "All right, let's try to climb up."

"Can you manage?" asked Torazo. "You don't look very good."

"You're not such a pretty sight yourself," retorted Zenta, grinning painfully.

It was true that the boy had never looked worse. His scraped and swollen left cheek was purplish and gave him a lopsided look. Tears had made furrows in his dusty face, like deep wrinkles. But he grinned back, for once quite undisturbed by the unflattering reference to his looks.

Zenta stood up slowly on the ledge, keeping a firm grip on the cherry tree, and looked down into the ravine. The sight made him sick again. The ravine went down and down. The little stream mentioned by the Ohmori samurai sparkled in the far, remote distance. Zenta closed his eyes and concentrated on breath control until he fought off the nausea. "I'm ready to climb now."

Torazo tested a small cherry tree above them and pulled himself up. "This will take our weight."

Zenta reached out for the branch, and suddenly stopped. "My swords! I dropped them into the ravine!"

There was a terrible silence. Finally Torazo said, "I'll try to look for them."

"No, it's hopeless," said Zenta dully. For the first time since entering the valley of the cherry trees, he was overcome by despair. A samurai's sword was his soul, and to lose his sword was worse than losing his land, his house, and all his money. Without his sword he was naked and defenseless.

Torazo cleared his throat. "If we get out of this alive, I'll ask my father to present you with a pair of our family swords."

Zenta was ashamed. Torazo's courage had not failed, despite the hopelessness of their situation, and Zenta knew he had to live up to the boy's example. He sighed and said, "Then let's work on getting out of this alive."

For Zenta the next hour was a grim struggle that brought back memories of a recurring childhood nightmare: he was climbing up a mountain of ice, only to slip back three steps for every two he climbed. He summoned all his reserves of will power in order to ignore the message his abused body kept sending him, that it would be easier and pleasanter to let go and slip down the ravine.

From time to time he spared a glance at Torazo climbing ahead of him. The boy was making progress and showed no trace of his usual clumsiness. Both of them made so much noise that if any Ohmori samurai were still lurking in the vicinity, he would not have failed to hear them. No enemy voice cried out in alarm, however, and it seemed that the Ohmori men had truly left.

Suddenly Zenta realized that he was no longer hearing the sound of Torazo climbing above him. The boy had disappeared from sight. For a heart-stopping moment, he thought Torazo had fallen into the ravine, but then realized that he would have seen him hurtling down. In a burst of joy he knew why he could no longer see Torazo: the boy had reached the top. The knowledge gave him a new surge of strength and lent speed to his scrambling. Even sooner than he expected, he struggled past the boughs of a tree to find himself looking at the top of the ledge. Torazo's face appeared, split in a wide grin that made him look like a minor devil from a lurid Buddhist painting of hell.

After Zenta pulled himself up to the road, he and the boy stood looking at each other, too spent to speak. Then Torazo said, "If my mother were to see me now, she would say…"

And Zenta joined in union, "You need a bath!" Whereupon the two of them whooped with hysterical laughter. Zenta winced and raised his hand to feel the back of his head. It was sticky with half-dried blood.

Torazo's face sobered at the sight of Zenta's bloody fingers. "How is your head?"

"Sore, but so are a great many other places," said Zenta. "We'd better forget our bruises and look for some wooden sticks to use as weapons, in case we meet any unfriendly faces."

He spoke lightly and tried to hide the desolation that swept over him momentarily at the thought of his lost swords.

Torazo's wooden practice stick was still on the ground where he had dropped it during the attack by the Ohmori men. Zenta soon found another stout stick. He swung it a few times and nodded. "This will do."

"Are we headed for any place in particular?" asked Torazo as they started up the mountain path.

"We're going to Bunkei's house," replied Zenta. "We'll be meeting your father and Matsuzo there."

"My father?" Torazo trudged on silently for a few steps and then added, "Do you think he'll be pleased with me?"

The wistful note in Torazo's question did not escape Zenta. "I think your father should be very proud of you. You kept your wits about you even when things looked very bad for us."

"My father has never had any reason to be proud of me before," muttered Torazo. "He says I'm ugly."

Zenta was becoming dizzy from the sun beating down on his aching head. He found a flat rock in the shade and sat down. "Why should your father care about your looks? He is no beauty himself. In fact you look very much like him."

"Do I really?" said Torazo, startled. After a moment he said, "But it's not just my ugliness. He's also disgusted by my clumsiness."

"I don't think you're clumsy at all," said Zenta. "Look at the way you were climbing up the ravine just now."

"I'll never be a good swordsman," said Torazo dejectedly. "My father says his samurai will not follow a leader who is as hopeless with the sword as I am."

There was no arguing with Lord Kawai's statement. It was perfectly true. Zenta sighed and rose creakily. "We'd better go."

For some minutes they marched in silence. On the previous day the clearing had been close to Bunkei's house; now it seemed as if they would never arrive.

"Tell me about your teacher, Itoh Kenzaburo," Zenta said. "You're frightened of him, aren't you?"

Torazo made no attempt at denial. "He was sarcastic about my clumsiness and said that I could do nothing right. He used to complain about me all the time to my father."

Zenta knew Kenzaburo's reputation. As a swordsman he was virtually without equal, but he was extremely proud of his fearlessness and independence. He probably took pleasure in being merciless toward the only son of a powerful feudal lord. Harshness could be an effective teacher — Zenta himself had learned much from a fencing instructor both harsh and cruel — but for a boy as full of insecurity as Torazo it could be devastating. Small wonder that Torazo appeared to be clumsier than he actually was.

But it still didn't explain everything. "Kenzaburo may be a harsh man, but he is still a great swordsman. Why did he tell you to keep your eyes on your sword blade during an attack?"

"But he didn't!" cried Torazo. He started to say more, but broke off and closed his mouth stubbornly.

"You can't tell me about it?" asked Zenta.

Torazo shook his head, his face acquiring a curiously mature look. "It's something I have to settle myself."

Zenta didn't press him. There was no time in any case, for they were approaching the clearing with the cherry trees, and beyond was the small bamboo grove. Zenta stopped and looked around at the vicinity of the inn very carefully. There were sure to be Ohmori samurai about.

Nevertheless, Zenta was hopeful of reaching Bunkei's house undetected, for most of the Ohmori men would be occupied with tending their wounded. Furthermore, the inn was the last place that Zenta and Torazo would be expected to make for — assuming they survived the fall.

They arrived at the maimed cherry tree in front of the artist's house without attracting attention. But they were brought up short by an unexpected sight: two visitors were standing at the entrance about to ask for admittance. One was a priest, and the other was a court lady dressed in a full brocade robe of shimmering colors. On closer inspection, the priest turned out to be Matsuzo.

As for the court lady, the ends of her robe were tucked into her sash, revealing muscular, unladylike legs below. When Zenta and Torazo approached, both Matsuzo and the court lady whirled around. For a full minute Torazo stared at his father, dressed in the robes of an imperial lady-in-waiting. Then he burst into peals of laughter.

11

"You are sure that none of the Ohmori men suspects we're here?" asked Matsuzo.

Bunkei nodded. "Haru says they are all resting quietly in their rooms, licking their wounds. She'll warn us if any of them goes outside."

"Is Lady Ayame at the inn?" asked Zenta. A wash and a change of clothes had helped to repair his battered appearance, but he still looked subdued. He was cast down by the loss of his swords, thought Matsuzo.

At Zenta's question, Lord Kawai said, "Lady Ayame was at the Noh performance. I especially asked for her attendance."

His proposal to marry Lady Ayame had not prevented her father from betraying him, but if this fact embarrassed Lord Kawai, he showed no signs of it. Dressed now in one of Bunkei's kimonos, he had lost none of his arrogance or his air of command. There was no longer anything even remotely comical about him.

Torazo, after his initial burst of laughter, had turned sober immediately. He now sat at his father's right hand, but a short distance behind, as befitting a respectful son. Matsuzo was struck again by the startling resemblance between Torazo and his father.

"Well?" asked Lord Kawai. "Is it safe to discuss our plans without being overheard?"

"It's safe, unless that snoop, Gonzaemon, is skulking around," said Bunkei. He rose and checked the hallway and windows.

"Who is Gonzaemon?" demanded Lord Kawai.

"He claims to be a cousin of the innkeeper's wife," said Bunkei. "I don't trust the fellow."

"I believe he is a very competent swordsman," said Zenta. "We can certainly use an extra sword on our side. Perhaps he can be bought."

Matsuzo noticed that at the mention of Gonzaemon, Torazo gave a start. Zenta apparently noticed the reaction also, for he kept his eyes on the boy as he spoke. But Torazo's face became impassive and he lowered his eyes.

Meanwhile Bunkei was explaining his distrust of Gonzaemon. "He makes love to the innkeeper's wife behind her husband's back. Even worse, he is totally insensitive to art. Why, he made fun of this painting!"

Following Bunkei's pointing finger, Lord Kawai turned to look at the painting behind his back. After a moment he said, "I don't blame him. This looks like a squiggle made by a child. A very bad-tempered child."

Bunkei's chest swelled and his face turned dark red. Matsuzo braced himself for an explosion. To his surprise, Bunkei managed to control himself and subsided. He contented himself with glowering at the warlord.

For the first time Matsuzo felt his respect for the artist slip. Bunkei would never have tolerated such an insult from an ordinary man. Had he been cowed, then, by Lord Kawai's rank? Perhaps the artist felt that it was his duty as a host to ignore insults from his guest.

Lord Kawai was completely oblivious to Bunkei's emotion. "This is my plan," he said briskly. "One of you disguise yourself and head north. Once out of Ohmori territory, you send word to my chief of staff, who is presently camped with my army less than a day's march away. Have him mobilize his forces and bring them to the border. We have enough men to overwhelm the Ohmori force."

Matsuzo thought Lord Kawai's plan reasonable. The warlord was too well known to be able to pass through the enemy, but he himself or Zenta would have a chance. He was just about to volunteer for the role of messenger when Zenta spoke.

"I think we should modify this plan. Lord Ohmori must be concentrating all his men in the north, because he knows the boundary there is the one closest to this valley. If you move your army there, my lord, you will have a bloody clash, with unnecessary loss of life."

Lord Kawai was unmoved. "The loss of life doesn't matter, so long as all the Ohmori family are wiped out. I don't care for traitors."

"An additional drawback to your plan," said Zenta, "is that you and your son will be on the wrong side of the enemy lines during the battle. Lord Ohmori can have you hunted down and killed before he faces your main army."

"Well, well, this is beginning to sound like a staff meeting" said Lord Kawai. "You see yourself as one of my chief officers, perhaps?"

Zenta looked unmoved by the warlord's remark. "Due to circumstances of your own making, my lord, you have been trapped in the valley by your enemies. Your staff consists of your son, a painter, and two penniless ronin. We're not much, but we are the best you have at the moment."

Lord Kawai stared at Zenta. "I recognize you now! You and your friend were the ones who enlivened our cherry-viewing party the other day. What are you doing here? Have you changed your mind about becoming my court jester? In our present situation, we can use a touch of comedy."

"I'm here because I'm working for your son," Zenta said coldly. "As for comedy, I hear that you and Matsuzo did very well by yourselves. You don't need any help from me."

Matsuzo felt that the conversation was not taking a useful turn. "How should we plan our escape, then?" he asked Zenta.

"One of us should still head north and try to get word to Lord Kawai's army," said Zenta. "Only instead of ordering them to meet us at the northern boundary, we ask the men to march to the eastern boundary of the Ohmori territory. We have a better chance of rejoining the army if we go east."

Lord Kawai looked at his son. "Since this is turning out to be a regular staff meeting, I should hear the opinion of my heir."

Torazo winced at his father's taunt, but he gave his reply in a steady voice. "I think Zenta's plan is good. But you will need both of these samurai to protect you. Since I am not much of a fighter, I can be more useful as the messenger."

"What have we here? A budding strategist?" Lord Kawai's words were sarcastic, but his eyes were thoughtful as he looked at his son.

"No, I don't think you can pass through the Ohmori men," Zenta told Torazo. "They know your face too well. Someone else should be the messenger."

Slowly, four pairs of eyes turned to look at Bunkei. The artist shrank back in a vain effort to reduce his bulky figure. "Don't look at me! I'd be hopeless as a messenger. I'm a lazy drunkard, and I'll forget your message..."

"If you succeed in bringing word to my army, I'll reward you by making you my court painter," said Lord Kawai. "You can paint every single folding screen in my castle."

Bunkei brightened at the warlord's words, and after a moment a cunning glint appeared in his eyes. "How about the sliding doors?"

Lord Kawai sighed. "Yes, you can paint the sliding doors, too."

"Good!" said Zenta. "Bunkei is a familiar figure in the valley, and he can move about without arousing suspicion. While he is bringing the message, the four of us will..."

He broke off at the sound of approaching footsteps. The door opened, and Haru appeared with a tray of food. "Please excuse the delay. It took me so long because I had to prepare all the food myself."

She set out a large plate of cold rice balls wrapped in seaweed and arranged some small dishes of pickles. "I didn't dare light the stove to cook hot food in case my stepmother or one of the maids became suspicious."

Lord Kawai, about to bite into a rice ball, paused and frowned. "You believe they would betray us to the Ohmori men?"

"The maids may not mean to betray you, but they don't know how to hold their tongues. As for my stepmother..." Haru stopped, and then said slowly, "She chooses whichever way is the safest and most immediately profitable."

"Helping us right now is certainly not the safest choice," said Lord Kawai softly. He looked curiously at the girl. "Why are you taking the risk of joining our side, then?"

Haru indicated Zenta. "This gentleman saved my life, and I will do anything he wishes. Since he has decided to help you, I will do so, too."

"Hm...very noble," murmured Lord Kawai. Then he smiled. "Of course your rewards will be all the greater if our side wins out, eh?"

"Haru is not thinking of rewards!" cried Torazo, who half rose in indignation. "She was kind to me long before she knew who I was!"

Lord Kawai looked at his son in amazement. "Ho, ho, what is this? A romance? You're precocious, my boy. You must take after me!"

Matsuzo could hardly contain his disgust. What a filthy mind the warlord had! Not for the first time he wondered if he and Zenta had chosen the right side. The Ohmori family, though treacherous, had at least shown sensitivity.

But Haru did not seem in the least embarrassed by the exchange between father and son. She even gave Torazo a faint smile as she started to gather the dishes and place them on the tray. With a slight shock Matsuzo suddenly realized that Haru and Torazo were almost the same age. She simply regarded the boy as a friend.

As the girl prepared to leave, Zenta said, "Haru, we shall need disguises to help us pass through Ohmori country. Would you be able to bring us some suitable clothes?"

"Some mountain priest outfits would be the best," said Lord Kawai. "We can wear deep basket hats that cover the whole head down to the shoulder."

"No, that won't do," said Zenta. "Practically every fugitive in history has disguised himself as a mountain priest. The Ohmori men will be suspicious as soon as they see a basket hat."

"We can be a troupe of traveling performers," suggested Matsuzo. "How about disguising ourselves as jugglers?"

Lord Kawai turned a cold eye on the young ronin.

"Can you juggle?"

"No, but..."

"Then keep your preposterous suggestions to yourself," snapped the warlord." I should think you would have had enough of playacting after the fiasco you made of the Noh play!"

"I wasn't solely responsible for the fiasco!" said Matsuzo hotly. "Things wouldn't have been so bad if you hadn't taken up the priests lines!"

Haru broke in hastily. "I can borrow some clothes from nearby farmers."

"That's the best!" said Zenta. "The simpler the disguise, the better our chances. We'll have to pass through several villages and one medium-sized town, and our aim is to attract as little attention as possible."

After the warlord, his son, and the two ronin had left, Bunkei looked thoughtfully at the piece of paper with Lord Kawai's message. If this were found on him by the Ohmori men, he could expect no mercy. They might even torture him for additional information on the fugitives.

And what would be the rewards of painting all the screens and doors of Lord Kawai's castle? Bunkei laughed shortly. The warlord knew nothing about art. He might even throw away all the screens after they were painted and then hire another painter, someone who knew only how to dazzle the vulgar with a lavish use of gold foil.

Lord Ohmori, on the other hand, was a man of taste and discrimination. He gave his patronage to the most outstanding artists, actors, and musicians of the day. Haru had said...

Haru! Bunkei suddenly remembered that Haru had chosen to throw her lot on Lord Kawai's side. The thought of Haru finally brought Bunkei to a decision. His art was difficult for people to appreciate, and without the kindness of Haru's family, Bunkei suspected that he would not be living in a cozy little house, with delicious meals regularly served. If he failed to take the message, Haru would never forgive him, and he would lose his snug home.

Bunkei sighed and began to gather items for his journey north. He suddenly stopped, his eyes drawn to the small bottles Haru had brought for serving sake. The others had been too busy changing into their disguises to touch the wine. Bunkei reached for two of the bottles and shook them. They were still quite full. Perhaps he should refresh himself before starting his strenuous and dangerous journey.

Lord Kawai stopped, lowered his hoe to the ground, and rubbed his shoulder. "I feel like an absolute fool carrying this hoe! Why do we need these implements, anyway?"

Zenta looked back. "We are carrying farm implements because we are supposed to be farmers," he explained patiently. "And they may turn out to be useful weapons."

The warlord tried a few practice swings with his hoe and threw it down in disgust. "We should have tried to get hold of some swords. Didn't that girl at the inn..."

"Haru," supplied Torazo.

"Ah, yes, your friend Haru," said Lord Kawai, with a leer at his son. "She said her great-grandfather used to be a samurai before he turned innkeeper. We could have taken his sword."

"A sword which has been in storage for some fifty years would need a lot of polishing before we could use it," said Zenta. "Besides, a farmer carrying a sword would look suspicious."

He took the sickle that was thrust into his own sash and handed it to Lord Kawai. "Why don't we exchange? You can have the sickle and I'll take the hoe."

The four resumed their trudging. They had been walking for only a few hours and were a long way from their destination, the eastern boundary of Ohmori territory. But Matsuzo already felt as if he had been on a journey for several months. He gritted his teeth. Another day of Lord Kawai's company might drive him mad. So far they had passed through one village without arousing comment, mostly because it was the time of day when the villagers were out in the fields. But they would soon approach a town where they planned to spend the night. Their disguises would be put to a severe test.

For himself Matsuzo would have preferred to spend the night out in the woods, even if it meant shivering on the cold ground. They would be less likely to attract attention. But one look at his companions convinced him that a more comfortable resting place was needed. From the way Zenta was frowning, Matsuzo guessed that he had a crashing headache. Torazo was already stumbling with fatigue — the climb up from the ravine had apparently taxed him to the limit. As for Lord Kawai, Matsuzo could imagine his reaction to the suggestion that he spend a night in the woods.

It struck Matsuzo that the warlord's gait was most unfarmerlike. "My lord," he said, "could you march in a less military manner? Remember: we're acting the part of farmers."

"I don't need any advice from you on acting," Lord Kawai said stiffly. "Your performance as the old priest this morning was nothing to boast about!"

"*Your* acting as the court lady was no polished piece of work, either," Matsuzo retorted. "Why did you wave your arms so much? When you had no reason to move, you should have kept still."

"How dare you speak to me like that?" shouted Lord Kawai. He reached for his sword and found himself whipping out the sickle. With a snarl of disgust, he jammed it back into his sash.

Lord Kawai's fury had the effect of restoring Matsuzo's good humor. He was beginning to feel hungry, for the cold lunch prepared by Haru had been meager, and he looked forward to a hot meal when they reached the town.

After they had climbed out of the valley of the cherry trees, the road had become flatter and the walking easier. They were approaching fertile farmland, which was now yellow with the flowers of the oil-bearing *nanohana* plant but which would soon be flooded to form rice paddies. Matsuzo was sorry that there were fewer cherry trees to be seen, although the scenery had its own charm. The mountains, slightly hazy in the afternoon light formed a dramatic background to the bright yellow flowers.

"Look, there's a shrine," said Zenta, pointing to a small vermilion *torii* gate in front of a pine grove. "We must be getting close to the town."

He stopped and looked worriedly from Lord Kawai to Torazo. "I think, my lord, that you and your son should speak as little as possible. Your manner of speech would betray you instantly as samurai."

Lord Kawai drew himself up haughtily. "Surely you will permit me to ask the landlord for service?"

Zenta shook his head. "It would be better if I did all the negotiating for our accommodations. I have spent some years traveling around the country mingling with commoners and I know how to speak like a farmer."

"Bah, in these filthy clothes, how can they take us for anything but farmers?" demanded the warlord. "Couldn't that girl have found us some clean clothes, at least?"

Matsuzo, who had also been disgusted when he put on the dirty, sweaty clothes Haru had brought, had seen the girl's wisdom. "It would look strange if we all appeared in crisp, clean clothes. People would ask if we were celebrating some festive occasion, and then we might have to treat everyone to wine. We'd be the center of a large party."

"I'm already the center of a large party," complained Lord Kawai. "A large party of fleas."

At the warlord's words, Matsuzo felt an itch develop between his shoulder blades, but he resolved not to give Lord Kawai the satisfaction of seeing him scratch himself. He soon forgot the itch, however, at the sight of houses appearing in the distance.

He shouldn't have drunk all that sake, thought Bunkei, mopping his forehead. Now he had to hurry. By the time he had finished both bottles, he needed a nap. The afternoon had been half gone before he started his journey.

His legs now felt as limp as boiled noodles from the unaccustomed exercise, and his throat was like a bed of gravel in a drought. How could he, a talented artist and a man of excellent sense have got himself involved with this affair?

But at least he was making progress. The steep climb had leveled out and he knew that he was approaching the northern boundary of the Ohmori territory. Once over the border, it was a simple matter to seek out Lord Kawai's general and deliver the warlord's message.

When he turned a corner and saw the roadblock, he knew that things were not going to be simple after all. Some half a dozen travelers were lined up awaiting questioning by the Ohmori samurai manning the roadblock. As Bunkei joined the line, he noticed that the travelers were not only questioned but thoroughly searched as well.

His own prepared story about visiting a sick friend was beginning to sound more and more feeble. After a brief debate with himself, he came to a decision. Stepping out of line, he pulled a roll of paper from his sleeve and approached one of the samurai. "Take me to Lord Ohmori. I have something to show him."

None of the inns in the town had the quiet elegance of the one run by Haru's family. The four travelers walked slowly through the main street until they came to an inn less shoddy than the rest. It even had a small gate and a bamboo fence, giving it some privacy from the passers-by.

"This looks almost tolerable," said Lord Kawai. "I don't mind putting up here if the maids are decent looking."

Even Torazo, who had been uncomplaining so far, turned to Zenta and said, "Yes, let's stop. I'm tired."

Zenta was tempted. But after reflection he shook his head. "No, this place looks too expensive."

"Too expensive!" sputtered Lord Kawai. "Who do you think I am?"

"You're a farmer," said Zenta, "and farmers don't patronize this type of inn."

"We have enough money," insisted Lord Kawai. "That girl Haru gave us plenty."

"We'd look too conspicuous here, and the innkeeper would remember us," said Zenta, turning away from the gate.

After a moment Lord Kawai followed reluctantly.

"You think Ohmori will send men in this direction?"

"Possibly not right away," replied Zenta. "But when he fails to find a trace of us in the north, he will immediately send scouts in every direction."

"I hope Bunkei gets through soon," said Matsuzo anxiously. "It would be disastrous if he is captured by the Ohmori men."

"Bunkei will get through. He is clever and resourceful when he wants to be." Zenta spoke with more confidence than he really felt. He was remembering the sake that they had left at Bunkei's house. The artist was very fond of wine. Even more disquieting was the anger he remembered on Bunkei's face when Lord Kawai insulted his painting.

But worrying did not help. And they had more immediate problems, one of them being how to prevent Lord Kawai's arrogant behavior from giving them all away.

Zenta stopped at a crowded, noisy inn, whose front was open to the street. "This is a good place," he said.

"You expect me to spend the night *here*?" asked Lord Kawai incredulously.

"Since it's large and crowded, we'll be less noticeable," said Zenta. "And besides, it commands a good view of the street in both directions."

He sat down at the edge of the raised floor, next to some travelers who were washing their dusty feet before entering the inn. Matsuzo joined him, as did Torazo. The boy sighed with relief.

After some hesitation, Lord Kawai sat down as well. He evidently appreciated the strategic advantage of being able to see down the street in both directions. "I want a fresh tub of water, not the same one the others are using for their feet," he told the serving girl.

"You'll get your turn, grandpa," the girl said cheerfully.

The warlord was so shocked by her familiarity that words failed him. The innkeeper approached and said, "How many in your party?"

Lord Kawai recovered his voice. "Four, and we want two of your best rooms."

"Look here, we arrived before you did," protested the traveler next to Zenta. He glanced contemptuously at the four 'farmers.' "My friend and I are merchants, and we are prepared to pay well."

"Unfortunately our best room is already occupied," said the innkeeper, bowing to the merchant. "But we do have another room free. It's very comfortable, and it overlooks the street."

"We will take that room!" announced Lord Kawai, in a voice used to command armies. Heads turned in their direction, and Zenta closed his eyes wearily.

The warlord's eyes flashed, and next to him Torazo bared his teeth. Father and son together presented a ferocious sight.

The innkeeper gulped. "Why don't you share the room? It's a very large room and can easily accommodate six."

Zenta thought it time to take out the bag of money Haru had given him. He jingled the bag. "If you will let us share the room, we'll show our gratitude by ordering a few rounds of the best wine here," he said in a conciliating voice to the two merchants.

"Oh, very well," said the first merchant. He seemed relieved that an ugly scene had been avoided.

As the two merchants dried their feet and stepped up to the inn, Matsuzo whispered to Zenta. "We must try to persuade those merchants to leave, somehow."

"I agree," said Zenta. "Merchants see a great deal of the world, and they would penetrate Lord Kawai's disguise quickly. I think I have an idea."

He turned to Lord Kawai and whispered, "My lord, please be patient and wait here. Matsuzo and I will join those merchants in the public bath and drop a quiet word in their ear. I think I can persuade them to go to another inn."

The outdoor mineral pool used by the guests of the inn was not crowded. Most of the guests were probably already at dinner. When

Zenta and Matsuzo arrived, the steam looked almost incandescent in the late afternoon sun and gave the illusion that the pool was boiling hot. But in fact the temperature of the water was perfect. The two merchants were the only other occupants of the pool. Giving them a friendly greeting, the two ronin stepped into the water. Zenta winced as all his bruises screamed in protest, but he forced himself to smile at the merchant. "I hope my uncle didn't startle you. He is a little overwrought and tends to talk wildly."

"Yes, he sounded exalted," said one of the merchants. "He was ordering people around as if he were a samurai."

Zenta lowered his voice confidentially. "I'm afraid that's one of Uncle Jiro's symptoms. Ever since he cracked his skull last year, he has periods when he imagines himself to be a high-ranking samurai."

"Er...did you say symptoms?" asked the merchant.

"He has spells of violence," said Zenta. "But don't worry: they never last long."

Ripples began to spread from the merchant as he washed himself nervously. "What form do these violent spells take?"

"You saw that sickle he had?" said Zenta. "He whips it out and slashes around with it like a sword. By the way, if he comes at you during the night, just give me a call. I know how to handle him."

"How often does he have these spells?" asked the second merchant.

"Not more than once or twice a night," Zenta assured him.

"You know, these spells may not be the result of his injury alone," said Matsuzo. "I think they are hereditary because I notice that his son..."

As if by spoken agreement, both merchants scrambled out of the pool and began to towel themselves dry. "I think the inn may be a little nosier than we'd like," said the first merchant. "Perhaps we should try another one."

"We passed a nice, quiet inn on our way over," said Zenta. "But it was too expensive for us. You merchants are lucky that you can afford a better inn than this."

After the merchants had hurried off, the two ronin laughed quietly. Zenta finally closed his eyes and relaxed in the bubbling hot spring. He could feel his pain and fatigue slough off. Even his headache was getting better.

Neither Zenta nor Matsuzo heard the comment of one of the merchants as the two men left the inn. "Isn't it funny that this old lunatic imagines himself to be a samurai, when a real one is staying in the next room!"

12
十二

What woke Zenta was a slight shaking of the floor. The construction of the inn was flimsy, and any movement caused the floor to shudder. The vibration was hardly softened at all by their mattresses, for these were the cheap, thin variety called "rice cracker mattress" by long-suffering travelers. In the course of the night, Zenta had awakened to alertness several times as various members of his party had turned over in sleep. This time, however, he realized that the movement had been caused by a guest in the next room.

Zenta's ears strained to catch every sound. A faint rustle of cloth indicated that the man was putting on his outer garments, and soon there was the slow hiss of a door being carefully slid open. Footsteps pawed in front of their door and then down the stairs. It seemed that the guest was leaving.

Zenta had not seen the guest at all. When he returned from his bath the previous evening, the man had already been served dinner in his room by the maids and had apparently retired to bed soon after that, for they had heard no sound from him the rest of the evening.

Well, the man probably had a long journey to make and needed an early start, thought Zenta, relaxing. Their own party had only a day's walk before they reached the eastern boundary, and they could afford to sleep a little longer. Torazo especially looked as if he needed the rest.

Zenta was just about to go back to sleep when he became aware that Torazo was quietly getting up. Moving very carefully, the boy opened the door and stepped out.

There could be several reasons why Torazo was getting up: he might need to use the privy, or he might be too cold and want extra covers. But Zenta thought it unlikely, for there was something furtive about Torazo's movements. On a sudden impulse, Zenta went to the window and looked down into the street.

The figure of a man stopped from the front door of the inn and walked up the street, the guest in the next room who was leaving early. As Zenta looked at the figure, he nearly exclaimed aloud in surprise: the guest wore the two swords of a samurai. There could be a perfectly innocent explanation, of course. As Zenta had told Lord Kawai, the inn which he had chosen possessed certain features of safety, and it was altogether reasonable that another samurai, accustomed to living with danger, would instinctively choose it rather than a more luxurious stopping place.

But then came the sight he had hoped he would not see: a second figure, smaller than the other, stepped out of the front door of the inn. Zenta had no doubt at all that for reasons of his own Torazo was following the samurai.

There was no time to be lost. Zenta snatched up the only weapon he had, which was the hoe, and ran noiselessly out of the room and down the stairs. He did not even stop to put on his sandals at the front door, but left the inn barefoot.

Outside, a morning mist made the houses in the town look insubstantial, as if the slightest breeze would blow them away. Already Torazo's figure was growing faint, and the samurai he was following was completely invisible. Zenta followed more by sound than by anything else. Barefoot, he made next to no sound himself.

The samurai was heading west, covering the same road they had traveled the day before. Soon Zenta left the last of the houses behind him, and he began to wonder how long this double pursuit would last. The silence and the mist began to give the pursuit a dreamlike quality.

It was getting brighter, and Zenta knew that the sun would soon pierce the mist, making concealment impossible. Suddenly he peered intently: Torazo was no longer in sight.

Fighting panic, Zenta told himself that Torazo and his quarry had probably turned off somewhere. He concentrated on listening. Very soon he was rewarded by the sound of voices coming from a little distance to the left. That was where the two had gone — to the Shinto shrine in the pine grove Zenta had seen the day before.

Lightly and silently Zenta ran up the stone steps leading to the torii gate, but instead of passing through the gate, he swerved aside to a large pine tree. The aged tree, circled by a sacred rope of rice straw, easily concealed him. It was not the first time he had found his slender build an advantage.

He was just in time. In the next instant, the sun's rays pierced the mist, striking the vermilion torii gate as if setting it ablaze. The light penetrated the pine grove and illuminated the two figures standing within. The two immediately turned their heads away to avoid the dazzling glare, but Zenta had time to see the face of the samurai Torazo had been following. It was Gonzaemon.

"I recognized your voice when you were speaking to the maids serving dinner in your room," Torazo was saying.

"So that was it," said Gonzaemon. After a pause he said, "Did you tell any of your companions that you knew I was staying in the next room?"

"No! I kept my promise to you and told no one that I knew you," said Torazo indignantly.

To Zenta the words could mean a number of disturbing things. Was the boy plotting behind his father's back?

Gonzaemon seemed to be reassured by Torazo's reply, for his shoulders visibly relaxed and he gave a pleased chuckle. "All right, tell me why you got up at dawn to follow me. By the way, why are you dressed like a peasant?"

Ignoring the second question, Torazo countered with one of his own. "When you were giving me lessons in swordsmanship, why did you tell me to keep my eyes on my blade during an attack? According to Zenta, it's the wrong thing to do."

Zenta gave a start. Then it was not Torazo's regular teacher, Kenzaburo, who had told him to do this, but Gonzaemon! What could have been the reason? Was it simply a sadistic desire to mislead the boy and increase his clumsiness? There could be a more sinister reason, and at the thought Zenta shivered with cold. In truth the ground felt icy under his bare feet, and the cold morning air found its way under his loose kimono.

"Well, well, you prefer to believe your new friend rather than your old one," Gonzaemon said lightly. "Do you think Zenta is right about the sword?"

"Yes, I do," said Torazo steadily. "Why did you mislead me?"

"What makes you think I was deliberately misleading you?" asked Gonzaemon, no longer carelessly, but with real curiosity.

Torazo was plainly unhappy with what he had to say. "I know that you have been kind to me, and it's possible that you didn't mean to mislead me during the lessons." He paused, and then burst out with the question tormenting him. "But why were you always so vague about the time for the lessons? More than once I had to wait for you when you didn't show up. And two nights ago, the uproar broke out over the broken cherry trees while I was waiting. I could have got into very serious trouble!"

Zenta finally understood. He now knew exactly why the cherry trees had been mutilated, and the cleverness and cruelty of the scheme stunned him. Torazo was in immediate danger.

Zenta stepped in front of the pine tree, and his shadow, thin and long in the morning sun, sliced into the ground between Torazo and Gonzaemon. The latter whirled around, his hand in his sword. On seeing Zenta, his face went blank with shock, but as he took in Zenta's appearance, he recovered and even smiled. "Another farmer, I see, and this one armed with a terrifying hoe."

Ignoring the taunt, Zenta said, "Perhaps I can answer Torazo's question as to why you kept him waiting so often. Your purpose was to let him be seen by the Ohmori men. You wanted it reported that Torazo was often seen lurking near the cherry grove in front of the inn."

Torazo made a small sound, but choked it off. Zenta could guess what he was feeling, for the boy was no fool and probably half expected what he was hearing.

Gonzaemon flashed his square white teeth in a broad smile. "Please go on," he said.

"Lord Ohmori was shocked by a series of incidents, involving vandalized cherry trees," continued Zenta. "Lord Ohmori had also heard that Torazo was a sullen boy and troubled."

So far Zenta had been speaking calmly, but now his anger began to smolder. "You helped to increase his anxiety! While pretending to help with his swordsmanship, you deliberately gave him advice that exaggerated his clumsiness. You wanted him troubled and unhappy!"

"Dear me, now why should I do that?" asked Gonzaemon.

"Because you wanted Lord Ohmori to think that Torazo mutilated the trees!"

"How do you know that he didn't mutilate the trees?" asked Gonzaemon. "The boy has mental problems, and he could have been relieving his feelings by slashing at the trees."

Torazo looked up with flashing eyes, but before he could speak Zenta said, "I *know* that Torazo is innocent of the vandalism."

Gonzaemon's lips curled derisively. "Why? Because he is the son of a powerful feudal lord?"

Zenta had regained control of himself, and he put a hand on Torazo's shoulder to steady him. "I know that Torazo did not handle the ax on the night the last cherry tree was injured. His hands were sticky with syrup and soy sauce from some rice cakes Haru had given him, but the ax handle was clean."

"I see," said Gonzaemon, nodding. He slowly drew his sword and said to Torazo, "I have nothing against you personally, you understand." He actually seemed anxious to justify himself in the boy's eyes.

"Of course," said Zenta. "You were only serving your master, Takeda Shingen."

Gonzaemon's eyes narrowed, but his grip on his sword did not change. "How do you know I serve Takeda?"

"By your actions, chiefly," replied Zenta. "Your aim is to subvert Lord Ohmori from his master, and the man who gains most from this is Takeda. I was stupid not to have realized this earlier. You said you were a mountain man and had never seen the sea. I should have remembered that Takeda's province of Kai was completely landlocked. Of the major warlords, he is the only one with no access to the sea."

"I was actually heading east to Kai to report the success of my mission," said Gonzaemon. He seemed relieved that all pretense had been dropped. "You can imagine my shock when I heard Lord Kawai's voice in the inn!"

"Lord Kawai is still alive because the actor recruited to murder him changed his mind," Zenta told him. "He began to worry about what would happen after the assassination. You see, he knew he might not be allowed to live and spread his story."

125

"The miserable coward!" Gonzaemon's square white teeth flashed in a grimace of pure annoyance. "I had my doubts about him from the start, but Ujinobu wanted to use him. My idea was to hire you as the assassin. Unfortunately Ujinobu went about his recruiting too clumsily."

Zenta suddenly remembered Ujinobu's glances at the screen in his bedroom during their first interview. "So it was you!"

"What do you mean?" demanded Gonzaemon.

"You were the person hiding behind the screen in Ujinobu's room!" said Zenta. He saw at last that the whole Ohmori family had been unconsciously following Gonzaemon's orders. This clever agent from Takeda Shingen had discovered the weakness in each of the Ohmoris and had exploited it. Zenta felt a flash of real hatred for this smiling puppeteer. Lord Ohmori, a man of elegant tastes, and Lady Ayame, a warmhearted girl of spirit — both had been persuaded into actions that could lead to dishonor and possibly ruin. Even Ujinobu would not have decided on treachery if it had not been Gonzaemon's hand behind the screen. "So it was you who put the whole idea of assassinating Lord Kawai into Ujinobu's head!" Zenta said.

"He is an easy person to manipulate," said Gonzaemon. "And so are some others."

"Yes, you love to manipulate people," said Zenta slowly. "You made it seem as if Torazo was the one who mutilated the cherry trees. Lord Ohmori, who prized cherry trees above human life, was persuaded to betray his overlord because he thought Torazo was the vandal." Feeling the boy's shudder, Zenta said, "Remember, Torazo, that you saw through him in time."

"That doesn't matter. I can still remedy the situation," said Gonzaemon pleasantly. "Well, all these preliminaries are now out of the way. You are both prepared, I hope? Isn't it better to be killed this way instead of in some sordid tavern brawl?"

Zenta knew that he had two advantages. The morning sun was behind him, while Gonzaemon had to face the sun and was already blinking at the glare. But more importantly, Gonzaemon was underestimating him. He could tell from the other man's smiling, confident face. Any samurai holding a sword would underestimate a farmer carrying a hoe.

Smiling back at Gonzaemon, he said, "Oh, yes, we are both prepared." And with that, he gave Torazo a violent shove that sent him first staggering and then sprawling. As the boy fell out of harm's reach, Zenta shifted his grip on the hoe.

Gonzaemon laughed with genuine delight. "Ah, you're going to fight. That's much better. To tell the truth, I've never enjoyed cutting down unresisting peasants."

The working end of the hoe consisted of a slightly convex blade, tapered and sharpened at the end, used for digging into the ground. Zenta knew that Gonzaemon would expect him to swing the hoe in a circular motion, as he would swing a halberd, and strike at his opponent with the sharp end. He encouraged this belief by holding the hoe lowered in front of him.

The swordsman's answer to a halberd or a spear was to close with his opponent, because the longer weapons could not be easily maneuvered at close quarters.

True to expectation, Gonzaemon jumped forward and slashed down. But instead of swinging his hoe, Zenta brought it straight up to meet the sharp edge of the descending sword. Wood was no match for tempered steel, and Gonzaemon's sword cut through the wooden handle and sent the head of the hoe flying.

Zenta had exchanged length for maneuverability: instead of a clumsy version of a halberd, he now had a wooden stick only a handspan longer than his opponent's sword. Before Gonzaemon could recover from his surprise, Zenta brought the stick down on his opponent's skull. If his foot had not slipped on the dew-moistened pine needles, the fight would have ended. As it was, the stick made a deep gouge down one side of Gonzaemon's cheek.

A lesser fighter would have left himself wide open after the pain and shock of Zenta's attack, but Gonzaemon managed to bring his sword up and cover himself against a return stroke. On the whole, Zenta had lost by the exchange, for his opponent was no longer underestimating him.

Breathing hard, the two men sprang apart as if by tacit consent to consider their next moves. Gonzaemon bared his teeth in a grin which contained not a trace of humor.

Zenta tried to measure his stick in comparison to Gonzaemon's sword. He had a desperate plan, but to execute it he had to know the length of his stick almost to a hair's breadth.

Suddenly he felt a dazzling in his eyes. But his back was to the sun! Then he realized that Gonzaemon was trying the classic trick of bouncing light from his sword blade into his opponent's eyes. Ducking his head to escape the glare, Zenta launched himself forward. Gonzaemon brought his sword down in a slashing attack, but instead of parrying, Zenta thrust his stick straight at his opponents throat. He felt something give horribly under his stick, and at the same time a streak of fire raced across his chest.

Zenta had miscalculated, but not by much. He found the Takeda agent stretched on the ground, his windpipe smashed in. Gonzaemon made a convulsive effort to sit up, then fell back and lay still.

Zenta finally looked down at his own chest and saw that Gonzaemon's sword had slashed through the front of his kimono. There was a cut diagonally across his chest from shoulder to waist, but nowhere was it deep. He closed his eyes for a moment in relief and then pulled up his torn kimono to dab at the cut.

"Are you hurt?" whispered a voice behind him. It was Torazo.

"No, it's just a scratch," said Zenta. "I was counting on my stick being longer than his sword, but they were closer in length than I thought."

Torazo was very pale. He glanced at Gonzaemon and quickly turned away. "Is he dead?"

When Zenta nodded, Torazo sat down on a rock and burst into tears. His violent sobs seemed to tear him apart. Zenta's first instinct was to murmur a few words of comfort. But he held back, knowing that he had to leave Torazo some dignity. Anyway, there was no comfort to give.

He was now able to guess the story. Gonzaemon had sought out the lonely, unhappy boy and pretended not to know who he was. On discovering that Torazo was worried about his swordsmanship, he had seized the opportunity to offer secret lessons.

Zenta could imagine Torazo's shock on discovering Gonzaemon's betrayal. But at least the shock hadn't come all at once. The boy must have suspected something, for on the night when the Ohmori men had nearly seized him as the cherry tree vandal, Torazo had told Zenta that he had private business to finish. Perhaps he had intended to ask Gonzaemon about his failure to keep their appointment.

The Shinto shrine contained only a shabby wooden hut for housing its *kami*, or spirit. But it had a device for catching rainwater and a stone basin where worshipers could rinse their hands and mouth in symbolic purification. Zenta took out a hand towel which had doubled as a headband. He dipped it in the basin, wrung it out, and brought it over to Torazo.

The boy had brought his weeping under control, except for an occasional sob. He accepted the damp towel from Zenta and wiped his blotched and swollen face, made even uglier than usual by his crying. Finally he gave a shuddering sigh and said, "He was kind to me. He was the first man who was ever kind to me."

When Zenta made no reply, Torazo cried, "How can I trust anyone? I can't even trust you, can I?"

"No, you can't," said Zenta. He found it extraordinarily painful to say this. He knew that in an instant Torazo's former trust and respect for Gonzaemon could be transferred to himself, but he could not permit it. It would not be fair to the boy.

Torazo's mouth quivered and his eyes watered again. "Then I have to go through life without a single friend?" he cried. It was the cry of a boy starved for affection. He had probably never had a loving gesture from either of his parents. "Are you saying that nobody can love or trust anyone else?"

"No, that's not what I'm saying," replied Zenta. "But for someone in your position, knowing whom to trust and whom to distrust is a very important skill. You must learn this skill, just as you learn swordsmanship and commanding your father's men."

"Then it's my position that prevents me from having friends," Torazo said bitterly. "I think I would rather live like normal people, and give my friendship freely."

Better than anyone, Zenta knew that friendship too freely given could lead to tragedy. He felt his throat tighten. "You have to make a choice, Torazo," he said. "If you wish to remain your father's heir, you must accept the responsibility. That includes the most painful care in bestowing your trust."

Torazo sat with his head bowed for a long moment. When he finally spoke, his voice was still husky from weeping, but it was steady. "Very well, I accept the responsibility."

Zenta sighed. "Good. Well, then, the first thing you should learn is that you cannot trust a ronin you met only four days ago."

Torazo smiled tremulously. "Knowing someone a long time is not always enough, either. My father trusted Lord Ohmori because he had known him for years. See where his trust has put him!"

"As I said, knowing whom to trust is not an easy skill," said Zenta. "Although in your father's case it wasn't exactly misplaced trust in Lord Ohmori that put him in this trap. It was his miscalculation about Lady Ayame. He thought that marrying her would protect him against Ohmori treachery."

"If an experienced warlord like my father can make such a serious mistake," said Torazo wonderingly, "then I have a great deal to learn."

Zenta grinned. "'Speaking of your father, we must think about going back. He might be shouting down the inn at the moment."

Torazo stood up. "We can't just leave him like this, can we?" He couldn't even bear to mention Gonzaemon's name.

"No, we'll have to bury him," said Zenta grimly. He was thinking more about the alarm that could be set off by the discovery of Gonzaemon's body.

He walked to the back of the grove and prodded the ground with his stick. "Fortunately the ground here is soft, because the only digging tool we have is a broken hoe."

The inn was in an uproar. A party of white-clad pilgrims, on their way to the five Zen temples of Kamakura, were stopping and asking for refreshments. Normally pilgrims received preferential treatment for it made innkeepers feel virtuous to serve guests bound on a holy journey.

Lord Kawai, however, had no intention of being kept waiting for his breakfast while a large party of pilgrims was served first. A generous bribe to the innkeeper would have settled the dispute in his favor, but Zenta was carrying all their money. The warlord had to rely on a commanding voice and a haughty manner to carry his argument.

Milling about the downstairs room at the inn, the pilgrims were hungry and were not impressed by either commanding voice or haughty manner. Many of them were people of means in normal life, and they were becoming tired of this loud-mouthed peasant haranguing them from the top of the stairs. They all carried long staffs, and some looked as if they were prepared to use them. The situation was potentially ugly.

Matsuzo stood behind Lord Kawai on the stairs, trying unsuccessfully to restrain him. His morning had started badly when he woke to find Zenta and Torazo gone. He had been sleeping too soundly to notice their departure, and the cause of his deep sleep was too much sake the night before. He knew that he should have copied Zenta's example and drunk sparingly. But it had been an exhausting day, and he had felt like celebrating their escape from the Ohmori men.

Now his head rang painfully from the shouting. Lord Kawai had drunk at least as much as Matsuzo. Perhaps that accounted for his very short temper.

"Crazy old fool," whispered one of the maids behind Matsuzo. She and another girl were folding away mattresses in the sleeping rooms.

"I heard that he imagines himself to be a high-ranking samurai," said the other girl.

Matsuzo realized that they were repeating the story that he and Zenta had told the two merchants. Perhaps the story could be useful again.

He approached Lord Kawai and said, "My lord, you must not lose your dignity and descend to the level of commoners by arguing with them. If you will return to your room, I shall persuade the innkeeper to serve your breakfast immediately."

"I don't care about my dignity; I just want my breakfast," snapped Lord Kawai. But he saw the sense of Matsuzo's words, and returned grumbling to his room. "You'd better hurry! And where are my son and your insolent friend?"

Where indeed, thought Matsuzo worriedly. But first, there was the matter of breakfast. He descended the stairs and sought out the leader of the pilgrims, a tall, barrel-chested man whose bass voice carried further than the rest.

Putting on his most persuasive manner, Matsuzo bowed to the man and said, "Sir, you must forgive my old Uncle Jiro. Since his head injury, he imagines himself to be a great warlord, and if he is not shown the proper respect, he becomes violent."

The pilgrim put his hand on his staff. "I'm not without experience in violence myself. If your crazy uncle tries anything, he'll get another crack on his head that may cure him!"

The last thing Matsuzo wanted was a clash between the pilgrim's staff and Lord Kawai's sickle. "Of course Uncle Jiro is no match for you," he said hurriedly. "But what he might do is smash all the rice bowls and overturn the soup pot. That would mean no breakfast for any of us."

This was a telling argument for the hungry pilgrims. Matsuzo hurriedly pressed his advantage. "You are all devout Buddhists and compassionate, especially toward the afflicted. Why don't you let the innkeeper serve breakfast to my uncle first? It won't take long, and afterward you can all eat in peace."

Matsuzo's politeness had its effect, and the anger left the pilgrim's face. "All right, your Uncle Jiro can eat first."

Lord Kawai reappeared at the top of the stairs. "Where is my breakfast?"

"Yes, my lord, don't worry my lord, your breakfast will be ready in a minute, my lord," said one of the pilgrims, and snickered.

At that instant, the front curtains of the inn parted, and Zenta and Torazo entered. It was clear from their shocked expressions that they had overheard the words of the pilgrim. Their eyes slowly swung up to Lord Kawai at the top of the stairs, and their jaws slowly dropped down in dismay.

Later, when the four were upstairs in their room eating breakfast, Lord Kawai was truculent. Instead of admitting that his overbearing manner threatened to expose them, he chose to take the offensive. "Where did you two go, anyway?" he demanded angrily. "Disappearing in the middle of the night like that!"

For once Matsuzo found himself allied with Lord Kawai. "I was frantic when I found you gone," he said to Zenta. "Why didn't you tell me where you were going?"

Zenta reached for the rice container. "You were fast asleep."

The curt answer annoyed Matsuzo, especially since he felt guilty at having slept so soundly. "Well, whatever your mysterious errand was, you two came back as dirty as a couple of dogs burying some bones."

Torazo choked on a mouthful of soup. Matsuzo saw that after the boy finished coughing, he exchanged a look with Zenta, who shook his head almost imperceptibly.

"We discovered that Gonzaemon was staying in the next room," began Zenta.

"What?" cried Matsuzo. He remembered Bunkei's remarks about the man. "Why, he could be a spy. If he found out that Lord Kawai was here, he might report us!"

Zenta calmly finished his second bowl of rice. "It seems that he was no common spy. He was an agent of Takeda Shingen."

Lord Kawai's face became thoughtful. "In that case he could be very dangerous to us."

"He *was* very dangerous so I killed him," said Zenta.

After he recovered from his shock, Matsuzo looked more closely at Zenta and realized that there was a great deal his friend was not saying.

Lord Kawai apparently felt the same. "And so you just killed him. With what? Your hoe?"

"That's right — with the hoe," replied Zenta. Both he and Torazo bent over their rice bowls and concentrated on eating.

Lord Kawai stared. "Well, if you're determined to put on the strong, silent warrior act, I won't press you. Perhaps Torazo can tell me what happened." He turned to his son. "Just what made you suspicious of the man in the first place?"

Torazo was attacking his broiled fish with his chopsticks, and he seemed determined to break it into tiny flakes. "I…I heard him speak last night, and I could tell he was a samurai. So when he got up before dawn this morning and crept out, I thought we should find out more about him."

"Hm… that was very alert of you," said Lord Kawai.

From Torazo's face, Matsuzo guessed that this was the first time in his life he had ever been praised by his father. He saw to his horror that Torazo seemed to be on the point of tears. Matsuzo's own family had been affectionate and close, despite their reduced circumstances, and he felt sorry for a boy who was moved to tears just because his father had said a kind word to him.

Zenta's next words took Matsuzo's mind from Torazo's distress. "Although Gonzaemon is dead, I'm still worried about him. He had discovered our identities last night, but instead of trying to report our presence to the nearest Ohmori samurai, he stayed in his room until nearly morning. What was his reason?"

It was a disquieting question, and Matsuzo could think of only one explanation. "Perhaps Gonzaemon thought we were all armed.

He was afraid that we'd kill him if he ventured out, and he only stole out of his room in the middle of the night when he thought we were all sound asleep."

"I agree that this may be why he waited so long before leaving the inn," said Zenta. "But I find it strange that he didn't try to smuggle out a message to the Ohmoris."

Matsuzo began to shovel rice into his mouth. "If Gonzaemon really did send out an alarm, we'd better start moving," he mumbled between mouthfuls.

Zenta shook his head. "If that's the case, rushing out of here won't be of any use, not with a mounted force after us. We'd better do something to change our disguises first."

However insufferable as a fellow traveler, Lord Kawai did not lack courage. He finished his breakfast unhurriedly and said, "I shall be glad to get out of these stinking rags. What do you suggest for our new disguise?"

"I think we should buy some white cotton clothes and join this party of pilgrims," said Zenta.

"Then I can carry a long staff," said Lord Kawai with satisfaction. "It will be a more suitable weapon than this sickle."

"I have weapons even more suitable for you, my lord," said Zenta, unwrapping a long bundle. "Here are Gonzaemon's swords."

Lord Kawai looked at the swords silently for a minute. His next action proved that it was not the accident of birth alone that made him a powerful warlord. Pushing the swords back to Zenta he said, "You'd better carry these. You can put them to better use than I can."

"No, my lord," said Zenta. "It is more in character for you to wear them. But I may borrow them if the need arises."

And Matsuzo knew that Zenta, too, was showing his true character. For he had not offered the swords to Lord Kawai out of deference to the warlord's rank. He had offered them because Lord Kawai was supposed to be a lunatic who imagined himself a great samurai. Therefore the pilgrims would not be surprised to see him wearing a pair of "dummy" swords.

Zenta's fears about Gonzaemon were well founded. One of the inn servants, recruited and well paid, had already gone off on the previous night with an urgent message from Gonzaemon to Lord Ohmori.

The message said that Lord Kawai, his son, and two ronin were disguised as farmers and were staying in the town overnight. From the snatches of conversation he had overheard, Gonzaemon thought that their plan was to head for the eastern boundary of Ohmori country.

13
十三

Lord Kawai's behavior was subdued from the moment they set out in the company of the pilgrims. Matsuzo glanced at him uneasily from time to time as they walked. He distrusted this meekness and was afraid the warlord was merely storing up his choler to release it later in one huge, catastrophic blast.

It was while the party stopped at a way station for lunch that Matsuzo discovered the reason for Lord Kawai's uncharacteristic restraint. As the tavernkeeper appeared to serve the travelers, the warlord began to demand service in his usual overbearing way. Immediately the pilgrims made way for him with exaggerated deference, addressing him as "my lord" and bowing low. There were smiles and giggles as several of the pilgrims nudged each other.

Although Lord Kawai would not hesitate to endanger his disguise by his arrogant behavior, he did have one weakness: he was sensitive to ridicule. When he saw the sly smiles of the pilgrims, he fell back at once to await his turn to be served.

Matsuzo was delighted. It seemed that they would be safe, for every time the warlord's behavior threatened exposure, the ridicule of the pilgrims would be enough to subdue him.

"Our problems are over," Matsuzo whispered to Zenta, as they ate their lunch in the small tavern. "We have only a short distance to go, and it doesn't look as if Lord Kawai will misbehave between here and the border."

Even Zenta sounded cautiously optimistic. "Yes, we're fortunate to fall in with this party of pilgrims. They seem to accept our story that we're joining the pilgrimage to pray for a cure for Uncle Jiro. My only worry is that Bunkei might be captured by the Ohmori men. But I think he is shrewd enough to get himself out of trouble."

Their peace was shattered by the sound of horses approaching at a gallop. Matsuzo felt his heart echoing to the hoofbeats, and his worst fears were realized when the horses stopped in front of the tavern.

The curtain was flung open and a helmeted samurai in Ohmori insignia strode into the room and looked over the company. Behind him were other armed men, blocking any attempt to escape.

"Have any of you seen a party of four farmers?" demanded the samurai.

The tavernkeeper approached and bowed. "We… have had a number of farmers stop here. Which particular ones do you mean?"

The samurai frowned impatiently. "You won't fail to notice these farmers; their behavior will be strange."

"I… I'm sorry, sir, I don't know what you mean," stammered the tavernkeeper.

The samurai pointed at one of the pilgrims. "You there! You have been on the road. Did you see a party of four farmers?"

The pilgrim stared dumbly and then turned to the leader of his party. The leader shook his head. "No, we haven't seen any farmers like the ones you describe."

Taking one last look at the white-clad pilgrims, the samurai turned on his heel and marched out. They could hear him giving orders to his men outside. "Hurry! We may still catch them on the road!"

The hoofbeats died away, and for a few minutes there was silence in the tavern. Then the leader of the pilgrims stirred. "These arrogant samurai — I hate them! I wouldn't tell them if the sun traveled from east to west."

He turned to Matsuzo, for whom he seemed to have developed a liking. "What did Uncle Jiro do? Say something rude to those samurai?"

"Er…yes," said Matsuzo weakly. "You know how he is."

"I certainly do," said the pilgrim, laughing. He rose and picked up his staff. "Well, it's time to leave."

The others quickly followed his example. As the leader passed Lord Kawai's bench, he said kindly, "Don't worry, my lord, you can behave any way you want to us, my lord."

Contrary to Matsuzo's expectation, Lord Kawai showed no sign of anger as he took his place in the line of marching pilgrims. He looked thoughtful. Finally he broke his silence and said quietly to Zenta, "I wonder why that pilgrim hates the samurai. Do all commoners feel the same way?"

"Probably," said Zenta. "The warrior class has done very little to endear themselves to the commoners."

"I wonder if the commoners in my territory feel the same way," mused Lord Kawai. "It can't be a very healthy state of affairs, and it must weaken the country."

Torazo, who had been listening to the conversation, said, "The Ohmori samurai may be resented more because the taxes are higher here. Lord Ohmori has expensive tastes."

"Where did *you* hear all this?" Lord Kawai demanded, amazed.

"Here and there," muttered Torazo, blushing. "Mostly from Bunkei and Haru, but also from farmers."

Lord Kawai stared at his son as if he had never seen him before. "So that's why you disappear all the time — you go around talking to all sorts of strange people!" But he did not look entirely displeased.

Matsuzo had more pressing worries than the hatred of the commoner. "It seems you were right about Gonzaemon smuggling out a message," he told Zenta. "Those men were asking specifically for disguised farmers. And now they're probably going to alert the border guards."

Zenta nodded soberly. "We can't possibly hope to cross the border undetected. Our only hope is that Lord Kawai's army will be waiting for us there."

"And that depends on Bunkei getting his message through on time," said Matsuzo. Bunkei might be delayed, but the possibility that the artist might not get through at all was something he refused to face. "What if we reach the border before Lord Kawai's army?"

Zenta shook his head gloomily. "It will be difficult if the rest of the pilgrims all pass through, leaving the four of us behind. We'll be as conspicuous as a troupe of jugglers on an empty Noh stage."

Matsuzo thought the reference to Noh unkind, but he saw Zenta's point. His worries were partially forgotten, however, as he watched Lord Kawai trying to strike up a friendly conversation with the leader of the pilgrims. In an effort to bring himself down to the other man's level the warlord put on a ghastly show of camaraderie. But he was genuinely interested in questioning the leader and obtaining his opinions.

For his part, the pilgrim was vastly amused by Lord Kawai and made a special effort to be gracious. After a while he even forgot that he was humoring a madman and began to present his genuine opinions. He was a widely traveled merchant and was well informed on a variety of topics, including politics and foreign trade.

The journey passed quickly — too quickly for Matsuzo, for it was clear when they arrived at the border station that there was no sign of Lord Kawai's army.

"What shall we do now?" Matsuzo whispered. The four of them had hung back until they were now at the end of the line of pilgrims. Already the pilgrims at the head of the line were approaching the checkpoint.

"They seem to be examining and questioning the travelers one by one," said Zenta. "Of course they will see right away that we are not normal pilgrims. But as long as they only hold us as suspicious characters, we can still hope."

As he spoke, Zenta scanned the guards at the checkpoint. "There are ten men, all fully armed, and an unknown number of men in the guardhouse. That inn over there may have more soldiers, possibly the ones who passed us on the road. I'm afraid we haven't a chance of fighting our way through, not with only one pair of swords among the four of us."

"The questioning is very thorough, but at least this means the line is moving very slowly," muttered Matsuzo. He felt an ache in his hands and realized that he was gripping his staff too tightly. "If only we had more time! What could have happened to delay Bunkei?"

He glanced at Lord Kawai and Torazo to see how they were taking the strain of waiting. If they felt any fear, they were concealing it well. Perhaps Torazo was pressing closer to his father than he had done before.

"Lord Kawai's army may still get here in time," said Zenta. "At this rate, it may be a while before we reach the checkpoint."

But there was less time than they had thought. Matsuzo heard the sound of distant hoofbeats, and he turned around to see a mounted party of about twenty men approaching at a furious gallop. His heart sank as the party reined to a stop in front of the line of pilgrims and he saw the face of the leading horseman. It was Lord Ohmori. Next to him, grinning in happy anticipation, was Ujinobu. A slight figure behind the two men pulled up, and for a moment Matsuzo did not recognize the face, although its elegantly chiseled features were familiar. Then he realized that it was Lady Ayame, dressed to ride as a warrior.

Ujinobu signaled his men to surround the party of pilgrims. "Knock off their hats, so we can take a good look at the faces of these pilgrims," he ordered.

But before the soldiers could obey, Lord Kawai stepped out of the line of pilgrims. "It won't be necessary to remove everyone's hat. I'm the one you are looking for."

As the soldiers closed in, Matsuzo heard one of the pilgrims exclaim, "That old lunatic was the real thing, after all!"

The two ronin were kept in a separate room from Lord Kawai and Torazo. They were treated well, even respectfully, but from the way their guards refused to meet his eye, Zenta guessed what their fate would be. "They will let us commit hara-kiri," he told Matsuzo. He wondered if Lord Kawai and Torazo had already done so.

Matsuzo did not look surprised. "When I left home, the only thing my father told me was that I should die well. I don't think he would be ashamed of me."

Zenta felt a keen stab of guilt. "I'm sorry. I never really gave you a choice. You don't even like Lord Kawai, and it's senseless to let you die for him."

Matsuzo shook his head. "There was no real choice. From the moment the abbot told us that we had to stop the assassination, we were no longer innocent bystanders." After a moment he smiled a little and added, "As for Lord Kawai, I began to dislike him less. He may be cruel, but he has nerve."

"If only we knew what happened to Bunkei!" said Zenta. It was hard for him to compose his thoughts for death when there was still hope.

The door opened, and the person who entered the room was the last one Zenta expected to see. It was Lady Ayame. Her military costume — pantaloons, puffed sleeves, lacquered cuirass, and arm guards — had the curious effect of making her look more beautiful and feminine.

Ever since he had discovered the treachery of the Ohmori family, Zenta's thoughts about Lady Ayame had been bitter. It seemed that her intervention on two occasions to save their lives had not been from kindness. She had saved them only because she thought she could employ them as assassins. Now that she had no further use for them, had she come to gloat over their fate?

But Lady Ayame's first words proved that Zenta's original impression of her was correct after all. "My father has agreed to spare your lives if you swear allegiance to our family and enter our service," she told the two men.

When surprise rendered Zenta speechless, Lady Ayame said impatiently, "You have no real loyalty to the Kawai family. When you blundered into the cherry-viewing party near the temple, it was Lord Kawai who ordered you killed, and it was I who asked him to spare your lives. You should reserve your gratitude to me, not to him!"

Her voice was warm and sincere, and Zenta found its appeal hard to resist. But her mention of the cherry-viewing party recalled other cherry trees, trees which had been savagely mutilated. "Lady Ayame," he said, "may I see the palms of your hands?"

She drew back. "What insolence is this?"

"Very well," said Zenta wearily. "I will tell you what I expect to see on your hands: new calluses, not those you've already had from handling the traditional weapons for warrior women. These new calluses are from handling an ax."

Lady Ayame studied her hands. "Go on," she said.

"We knew that the cherry tree vandal was someone short," said Zenta. "The suspicion was supposed to fall on Torazo, a moody boy known to avoid company and to wander around by himself at night."

Lady Ayame raised her head, and in her eyes there was real curiosity. "I still don't understand why you decided to champion Torazo. You had absolutely no reason to!"

"But I had a very good reason: I *knew* Torazo was innocent," Zenta told her. "That was why I began to look around for someone else who was short. It occurred to me that a woman could cut the cherry branches, especially a woman trained in arms."

Instead of attempting denial, Lady Ayame said, "What other reason did you have for suspecting me?"

"I heard the innkeeper's wife telling her stepdaughter to mend a torn sleeve for you," replied Zenta. "At the time I wondered how a lady could tear a sleeve at a peaceful cherry-viewing expedition. Once I began to suspect you, of course, I saw that the sleeve could have been torn by a falling branch. You also had ample opportunity. Since ladies never attend drinking parties, you could move about freely while the men were having their nightly carouse. You collaborated with Gonzaemon to dupe your father into thinking that Torazo was the vandal. You wanted your father to betray his overlord!"

Zenta looked around at Matsuzo, and he read consent in his friend's eyes for what he was about to say.

"I'm afraid we can never swear allegiance to your family. It would be too shameful."

Lady Ayame suddenly covered her face with her hands. After a moment she looked up fiercely. "I had to do it! I was being forced to marry Lord Kawai, and I loathed him!"

Her loathing of Lord Kawai was no surprise to Zenta. He had seen the revulsion in her eyes when she flinched away from the warlord during the cherry-viewing expedition.

"Couldn't you have found another way of avoiding the marriage?" he asked gently.

"How?" she demanded. "Was Lady Sayo able to avoid her marriage? Look at her now. She is counting the days when she can retire to a nunnery. That is what marriage to Lord Kawai has done to her!"

"You could have entered a nunnery, too," said Zenta. "That is preferable to the way you have chosen." But even as he spoke, he knew that religious life would be intolerable to this proud, spirited girl.

Her next words proved it. "I could never live in a nunnery. I want to do things! It's so unfair that Ujinobu will succeed my father. In everything except war, I can be a better lord to the Ohmori clan than he can ever be!"

It was not an idle boast. Even in war, Zenta suspected, she would make a better leader than her brother. This girl had the heart of a

142

warrior. But he was still unable to forgive her. "Your loathing of Lord Kawai I can understand, but why does Torazo have to be killed as well? He has never harmed anyone in his life — except himself."

"Ujinobu promised that Torazo would be kept prisoner, not killed!" Whether she truly believed her own words, Lady Ayame's present anguish was real enough. "I don't want any more deaths!" She was openly weeping now and tried to pull up her sleeve to mop the tears. Finding her sleeve tightly wrapped by the arm guard, she wiped her eyes with the back of her hand.

Zenta realized that she was trying to justify her actions — not to him, but to herself. Her offer to save their lives was an attempt to lessen her burden of guilt. But the guilt would never be lifted, and however powerful the Ohmoris became, she would always suffer from the knowledge of her family's treachery. Her lustrous hair, which had been coiled up for riding, now tumbled down in disorder about her shoulders, and her flawless skin was smeared and blotched with weeping.

Zenta's heart ached for her. He had never pitied anyone so much in his life, not even Torazo, who at least did not have to reproach himself. Beside him, Matsuzo made a rustle, and Zenta saw that his friend's eyes were also filled with pity for the girl. Their own position might be hopeless, but neither one would want to exchange places with Lady Ayame.

The door slid open with a crash, and Ujinobu marched into the room. He looked disgustedly at his sister. "You're making a spectacle of yourself, and the men will talk. Well? What do they say?"

Lady Ayame's voice was muffled. "They refuse to enter our service."

Ujinobu smiled. "Good. And you can stop your sniveling. It's their own choice, after all."

Zenta cleared his throat. "Lady Ayame, I do have one last request. Since you do not indulge in senseless cruelty, I believe you will grant it."

"What is it?" demanded Ujinobu before his sister could speak.

"There is no reason for our friends to suffer," said Zenta. "Bunkei, the artist, is just a harmless acquaintance. I hope you'll spare him."

Lady Ayame looked surprised, but she agreed readily. "Of course. I shall see that he is not molested."

"That artist may be harmless, but he is a madman and a confounded nuisance!" said Ujinobu. "He came up to us and tried to sell us a painting!"

"Oh? When was that?" asked Zenta, making a supreme effort to sound casual, but the surge of hope that went through his chest was almost painful.

"It was when we were hunting for you at the northern boundary yesterday evening, and our men were questioning all the travelers who were passing through." Ujinobu shook his head over the bizarre incident. "One of the travelers was this artist, and he insisted on seeing my father to sell him a painting! We couldn't kick him across the border fast enough. And the painting was just a senseless squiggle!"

Zenta's eyes met Matsuzo's. Bunkei had succeeded in crossing the border to Kawai territory yesterday! Even allowing for his delay in finding Lord Kawai's general, it seemed likely that the army might reach the eastern border very soon. They still had a chance!

Zenta tried to school his expression, but he was afraid that his face betrayed the same excitement he saw mirrored on Matsuzo's face. Ujinobu did not fail to notice their exchange of glances. "What has happened? You know something!" When the two ronin remained silent, he frowned suspiciously. "Does it have something to do with the artist? Answer me, or I'll have the guards beat an answer out of you!"

Lady Ayame looked at her brother in amazement. "What do you mean?"

At that moment the door opened and a samurai entered. "Lord Kawai has agreed at last to commit hara-kiri and requests that these ronin act as seconds for himself and his son."

To Zenta's relief, the news distracted attention from Bunkei. "Good!" exclaimed Ujinobu. "The cunning old badger tried to stall for time, I could tell. But he has evidently given up now." He grinned at Zenta. "After we're through with Lord Kawai and Torazo, we can arrange something for you, eh?"

As the two ronin left their room under escort, Zenta tried to hide his elation. The warlord's request offered a solution to a problem worrying him. The problem was that when Lord Kawai's army came into sight, the Ohmori men might fall on the prisoners and slaughter them before they could be rescued.

But acting as a second during the hara-kiri ceremony would put a sword into Zenta's hands, for his duty was to strike off Lord Kawai's head after the latter plunged his knife into his abdomen; the purpose of the act was to shorten the suffering, since one did not die immediately from disemboweling. A man committing hara-kiri was permitted to choose anyone he wished for his second — usually a friend or a master swordsman. Lord Kawai's request for Zenta as his second was therefore a calculated insult to the Ohmori samurai as well. Zenta's respect for the warlord grew.

They were brought into a courtyard of the border station. In the middle of the courtyard, two tatami mats had been placed together on the sandy ground to form a square. Lord Kawai and Torazo sat on the square, flanked by Lord Ohmori and his men seated on two sides of the courtyard. In one corner of the courtyard was a magnificent old cherry tree, whose petals floated down slowly on the assembled company.

Zenta could see irony in the scene. Only a few days ago, Lord Kawai had jokingly ordered a score of men to commit hara-kiri on a cherry-covered hillside. Now he himself was seated under a cherry tree, waiting to be handed a knife for this very purpose.

Both Lord Kawai and Torazo wore white silk kimonos, the robes of death. They were more composed than Lord Ohmori and his men, who looked strained and unhappy. Loyalty was the primary virtue of a samurai, and what they were about to witness was the final act in their betrayal of their overlord.

Lord Kawai beckoned Zenta and Matsuzo to approach. When they were close enough not to be overheard, he whispered, "Do you think there is hope that your artist friend got through? I've been stalling as long as I could, but Ohmori is becoming impatient. If I don't kill myself soon, they will do it for me."

Zenta bent forward to hide his smile from the Ohmori men. "My lord, we know that Bunkei crossed the border yesterday evening."

Lord Kawai gave a start, which he quickly transformed into a shrug of defeat. "How did you find out?"

"It was from something Ujinobu said," Zenta told him. "Your army may arrive at any moment."

Torazo passed his hands over his face to wipe off the smile that threatened to break out. "How can we stall for more time? We've already had a long bath and changed into these clothes. My father took his time shaving and even I asked for the use of the razor." His eyes were impudent as he rubbed his smooth cheeks.

Zenta grinned at the boy. At first he had only pitied Torazo, and later he admired the boy's courage. Now he felt the beginnings of affection. He turned to Lord Kawai. "We had better acquire some weapons as soon as we can. My lord, announce that you are ready. Then I can ask for a sword."

While Lord Kawai was announcing his readiness, Ujinobu and Lady Ayame arrived and took their places among the spectators. The girl did not look like a willing spectator and was probably there at her brother's insistence. Ujinobu was the only person present who seemed pleased with himself.

With great deliberation, Zenta tied up his sleeves, making sure that all the folds and wrinkles were adjusted to his complete satisfaction. His ears strained in vain to hear the sound of arriving troops.

"That's enough fussing," said Ujinobu impatiently. "Give him a sword, somebody."

Zenta examined the first sword offered to him and shook his head. "This has a very poor edge. Don't you have anything better?"

"He's trying to delay us," growled Ujinobu.

"I'm trying to obtain the best sword I can," explained Zenta. "After all, it is for your overlord. But perhaps this is the best that the Ohmori clan can offer."

"He can use mine," said Lord Ohmori, handing his sword to an attendant. He was very pale.

Zenta took the sword from the attendant and examined the blade with a low murmur of admiration. "A beautiful piece of work, my lord. May I know its history?"

But even Lord Ohmori was losing patience. "Let's just say that this is the best sword the Ohmori clan can offer. Shall we proceed?"

There was still no sound of an approaching army. Two wooden trays were brought, each containing a sharp knife, and they were placed in front of Lord Kawai and Torazo.

"What now?" asked Lord Kawai. "I don't hear any sound of my men."

Since these were also Zenta's thoughts, he had no answer. He racked his brain to say something reassuring, for he could see that

Torazo was staring at the knife on his tray with sick fascination.

Matsuzo leaned over. "My lord, you can ask for ink and brush to write a farewell poem," he whispered. "Many great warriors have written famous death poems, and I'm sure that Lord Ohmori will grant your request."

"Nonsense!" said Lord Kawai. "Ohmori knows perfectly well that I never write poetry. The request will simply make him suspicious."

"Perhaps you can put on a show of reluctance to proceed," suggested Zenta.

Lord Kawai looked outraged. "Certainly not! If I were genuinely committing hara-kiri, I would not show the slightest reluctance!"

"Can't you at least pretend?" begged Zenta.

"I'm not an actor!" said Lord Kawai.

"I knew you were not an actor when I saw you on the Noh stage," said Matsuzo unforgivably. "But you can at least try."

The Ohmori men were growing visibly restless at the prolonged whispering. Ujinobu half rose in his seat. "I'm convinced that they have no real intention of committing hara-kiri. Let's just cut them down and not waste any more time!"

There was still no sign of Lord Kawai's army.

Zenta heard a sobbing breath from Torazo, and saw to his horror that the boy was reaching for the knife on his tray. "All this is partly my fault, anyway," Torazo said. He managed a smile, although his lips were white. "Father, let me go first."

A moan came from the watchers, and Zenta turned around to see Lady Ayame falling over in a dead faint. The prospect of witnessing Torazo's death had apparently proved too much for her.

In the confusion following Lady Ayame's collapse, Zenta finally heard the long-awaited sound of galloping horses and the tramping of many feet. Challenges were shouted and peremptory answers rapped out.

The Ohmori men jumped to their feet in alarm. A white-faced samurai rushed into the courtyard and bowed down to Lord Ohmori. "My lord, an army has arrived. They…they are carrying Lord Kawai's banners!"

Zenta stood up. "Lord Ohmori, you have less than fifty men here. Resistance is useless."

Ujinobu's face was contorted with fury. Drawing his sword, he

147

sprang at Zenta, his cowardice for once overcome by his hatred. "The army will be too late to save you!"

Zenta sidestepped the attack, swung the Ohmori sword, and cut off Ujinobu's head with a single stroke.

Before the rest of the courtyard could recover, Lord Kawai rose, holding the wooden tray with the knife on it. Offering it to Lord Ohmori, he said, "I don't think I'll have any use for this. Why don't you take it instead?"

14
十四

They were back in Bunkei's house, sitting in the comfortable room that opened out to the bamboo grove. Again Matsuzo and the artist were drinking sake and discussing art — that is, Bunkei was discussing art and the young ronin was listening. It was as if the events of the last few days had never taken place.

There were minor differences, of course. The cherry trees outside were no longer heavily laden with blossoms, but here and there showed the tender green of new leaves. Another difference was that Zenta was not at his normal occupation of polishing his swords. He had none to polish.

Listening to Bunkei's discourse on brush techniques, Zenta had a sudden thought. "By the way, why were you trying to sell a painting to Lord Ohmori? Didn't that call attention to yourself unnecessarily?"

Bunkei smiled and poured more sake for Matsuzo. "That was my whole intention. You see, they were searching all the travelers very thoroughly, and I had Lord Kawai's message pasted to the underside of my painting. If I had shown the slightest hesitation in producing the painting, they would have examined it carefully and found the message. Therefore I insisted on showing it to Lord Ohmori and his family. I made such a nuisance of myself that they couldn't wait to throw me out."

Matsuzo looked horrified. "You were taking a terrible risk! What if Lord Ohmori actually wanted to buy the painting?"

Bunkei looked at the young ronin affectionately. "It's nice of you to say so, but I don't think there was any real danger of that. People don't seem to understand my work."

"So much the worse for them!" declared Matsuzo stoutly. "In time your genius will be recognized. I know it."

"Don't forget: you will be painting all the folding screens in Lord Kawai's castle," Zenta reminded the artist.

"And all the sliding doors, too," added Matsuzo.

Bunkei had the grace to look embarrassed. "He only agreed to that under pressure. I dare say he has forgotten all about his promise. Great warlords have a tendency to be forgetful."

"I agree!" said Matsuzo. He said to Zenta, "Lord Kawai should have let you keep the Ohmori sword, at least. You lost yours in his service, and Torazo promised that you would be given another pair."

Zenta said nothing. The loss of his swords still depressed him, but he had not expected to keep the Ohmori blade. After all, it was the family heirloom of a feudal lord and was not something lightly given away to a penniless ronin. Perhaps Torazo would remember his promise in time, but it would be foolish to count on it.

After the arrival of Lord Kawai's army, there had been a moment when violence threatened. A few of the Ohmori men attempted resistance, but it had died out when Lord Ohmori killed himself.

Finding Torazo too dazed to say anything and Lord Kawai busy issuing orders for the disposal of his enemies, the two ronin felt themselves superfluous. Without anyone noticing their departure, they left the border station and began to make their way back to the valley of the cherry trees. They had come to enjoy cherry blossoms, and this was what they would resume doing.

Haru's welcome had been a tearful one, for she confessed that she had not expected to see them again. The inn was quiet and peaceful. Not only were the guests gone, never to return, but the innkeeper's wife had disappeared as well.

"She probably went off to join her so-called cousin Gonzaemon," said Matsuzo. "She will spend a long time searching for him."

Haru had wanted them to stay at the main house of the inn, but both Zenta and Matsuzo preferred to stay on with Bunkei, whose company they enjoyed more than that of the obsequious innkeeper. Why should they move, when they were served the best food and drink the inn had to offer? They had nothing to do except relax, enjoy the poignancy of falling cherry blossoms, and talk about the ingratitude of great warlords.

"I'm surprised that Lord Kawai has not rewarded you," Bunkei said to Zenta. "You saved his life and that of his son."

Zenta shrugged philosophically. "He knew perfectly well that we didn't do it for his sake. And after all the embarrassing things we experienced together, he must be glad to see the last of us."

A malicious smile broke out over Matsuzo's face. "I'm sure he doesn't want any reminder of his disastrous Noh performance."

Zenta felt the beginnings of laughter bubbling inside of him. "And he knows I won't forget the time the servant girl told him, 'You'll get your turn, grandpa!'"

"I think it was the 'grandpa' part that really hurt," said Matsuzo.

"When was that?" Bunkei asked eagerly.

Zenta told him of their experience in the ramshackle inn, and of the pilgrims who bowed and scraped with exaggerated reverence every time the warlord opened his mouth. Bunkei roared with laughter when Zenta described the two merchants frightened away by the threat of Uncle Jiro creeping up on them at night with a sickle.

"And so you see," said Zenta, "it wouldn't surprise us if Lord Kawai never wants to see either of us again!"

In this he did the warlord an injustice. Even before their laughter subsided, the door opened and Haru appeared with a startling announcement for the two ronin. "Lord Kawai is back at Sairyuji Temple, and he has sent word that he wants to see you."

"I suppose that doesn't include me?" asked Bunkei, without much hope.

Haru's dimple played irresistibly in her cheek. "No, but he did say to tell you that he hasn't forgotten about his screens."

The warlord's messenger was one of the samurai who had arrived with the army. His greeting to the two ronin contained curiosity, mixed with some awe.

As they set off together toward Sairyuji Temple, Zenta asked the messenger, "Do you know what has happened to Lady Ayame?"

The answer was brief. "She has been sentenced to be executed."

Zenta was not surprised. The death of her father and her brother had left Lady Ayame completely crushed, and she might have obtained leniency if she had shown herself repentant. As soon as she had recovered her spirit, however, she had shown nothing but defiance. Matsuzo seemed to read Zenta's thoughts. "There is nothing we can do for Lady Ayame, not after she told Lord Kawai to his face that she joined the conspiracy because she didn't want to marry him."

Zenta nodded bleakly. Lady Ayame's fate was sealed. But he could not forget that she had twice saved his life. She had done her utmost to prevent unnecessary bloodshed. The memory of her tearful face during their last interview with her gave him an indescribable pang.

The main hall at Sairyuji Temple was being used by Lord Kawai as his reception room. Seated in the place of honor with Lady Sayo and Torazo on either side of him, the warlord was chatting affably with his officers when the two ronin entered.

As the two men bowed to him, Lord Kawai said, "Ah, you thought, didn't you, that your crazy Uncle Jiro had forgotten all about you?"

When the laughter died down, the warlord said to his son, "Well, Torazo, aren't you going to greet your cousins?"

Torazo smiled at Zenta, and in his smile was a new self-confidence. "My father is right: if he is your Uncle Jiro, then I'm your cousin."

Zenta understood what Lord Kawai was doing. The warlord knew that there were rumors about his undignified escape from assassination. Rather than wait for the rumors to gain in color, he was now choosing to tell the story himself. By deliberately exaggerating the comic details, he was making it sound like a rollicking adventure.

At the end of his story, Lord Kawai's face became serious. "My son told me that you dropped your swords into a ravine when you were rescuing him," he said to Zenta. "He will give me no peace until I present you with another pair. Yesterday, I saw Lord Ohmori's sword in your hands. I would have let you keep the sword but for the fact that it was too good for a ronin of no rank."

He paused, and let the silence stretch before continuing. "However, I have a solution to this difficulty: I can confer on you a rank suited to the sword. If I give you the income for fifteen hundred men, will you build a fortress here and hold the valley for me?"

It was a magnificent offer. Whatever personal faults the warlord had, he was not niggardly with his rewards. Among the thoughts whirling through Zenta's mind, one was dominant: if Lord Kawai was prepared to be this generous, perhaps he would be merciful as well.

152

Raising his head, Zenta said, "My lord, I am overwhelmed by your generosity. However, may I ask for a different favor?"

Lord Kawai's eyes narrowed. "What is it?"

"May I beg you to spare Lady Ayame's life?"

The warlord's face became suffused. When he finally spoke, the words sounded strangled. "I do not grant your boon."

To press the warlord further was to court disaster but Zenta had to make the attempt. "Lady Ayame saved my life. Even Haru, the innkeeper's daughter, repays her debt of gratitude. I can do no less."

From Torazo came an audible gasp. Zenta looked at Lord Kawai's face and saw that he had gone too far. Not only had he failed to save Lady Ayame, but he had made the warlord an enemy for life.

Support came from the last source Zenta expected. "My lord," Lady Sayo said, "the execution of Lady Ayame would look like the petty vengeance of a rejected suitor. I know that you really wish to spare her life, but you are prevented by the fear of appearing weak. Therefore, granting this boon gives you a good excuse to show mercy."

Lord Kawai turned his head slowly and stared at his wife, who met his gaze unflinchingly. "Don't try to be clever with me," he told her coldly.

When he looked back at Zenta, his face was totally without expression. "Your boon is granted: Lady Ayame will not be put to death. But I suggest that you get out of my sight as soon as possible."

When the doors of the reception hall closed behind the two men, Matsuzo blew out his breath gustily. "I know you have to keep up your reputation for recklessness, but before you do something like that again, give me a chance to crawl under a tatami mat first!"

Zenta's smile was a little shaky. "I should have consulted you first before turning down all that wealth and rank in exchange for Lady Ayame's life."

"I wasn't expecting wealth or rank, anyway" said Matsuzo. "But have we really saved Lady Ayame? Old Uncle Jiro back there might still arrange an accident for her. He hates to be balked."

Zenta had an idea. "Let's go see the abbot. He has many social connections, and he would be able to do something to keep her safe."

The abbot needed no persuasion, and agreed immediately to ask a relative of his in the capital to provide shelter for Lady Ayame. Leaving the abbot's quarters, the two ronin were met by a female attendant. "Lady Sayo would like to see you in her room," she said, bowing.

"I'll have to thank her again for helping us," Zenta whispered to Matsuzo, as they followed the attendant. "It's becoming a habit."

Lady Sayo, however, was not waiting to receive their gratitude. She dismissed all her attendants, and when she was alone with the two men, she reached behind her and brought forward a long bundle wrapped in a piece of dark silk brocade. "I want you to have this," she said, offering the bundle to Zenta.

His hopes rose, for there was no mistaking the shape of the bundle. With gentle fingers, he folded back the cloth and looked down on a pair of swords.

"I brought them with me as part of my marriage portion," said Lady Sayo. "They are supposed to pass down to Torazo when he comes of age, but I am giving them to you. Torazo has agreed."

For a moment Zenta was unable to speak. "You had no need to do this," he said unsteadily. "Any sword with a good blade would have been sufficient."

Lady Sayo did not reply immediately. Zenta glanced up at her and saw that she was somehow different. He realized that her harsh features had softened, making her look years younger. "I want you to have these swords because they belonged to my father, and you resemble him," she said. "You even sound like him. That day when I overheard you speak in the next room, it was like hearing my father again."

She smiled faintly, and Zenta caught a glimpse of the happy girl that she had been before her marriage, before the cold, watchful look settled in her eyes.

Once again Lady Sayo looked at Zenta in the searching way he remembered. "Can't you tell me your parentage?" she asked. "It may even be that we are related."

Zenta shook his head. The subject of his family was intolerably painful to him, and he would not discuss it with anyone, not even Lady Sayo.

She sighed. "Whatever else, I shall always be grateful to you for having saved Torazo, and it was not only his life you saved but also his honor. Do you know that even I suspected him of being the cherry

154

tree vandal? I was at a loss to account for his constant disappearances!"

Zenta had no intention of explaining that Torazo's disappearances had been caused by Gonzaemon's plot. It would be too humiliating for the boy if the truth were known.

Lady Sayo roused herself to more immediate business. "We are talking too long here. My lord remembers insults, and you have insulted him in public. It is time for you to leave."

"Lady Sayo was right" said Matsuzo. "It was time for us to leave. Did you see those guards at the gate? They backed away from us as if we had a loathsome disease."

The two men were leaving Sairyuji Temple and passing through the valley of the cherry trees for the last time. Too proud to run, they were nevertheless walking at a brisk pace, for it was not prudent to linger. Gradually, they became aware that someone was following them.

Zenta sat down on a rock by the wayside and waited. Because he had been half expecting it, he was not surprised to see Torazo's figure approaching.

The boy walked up to the two ronin and stopped. "I just want to say that in two years I shall be grown," he announced. "And then I can choose my own friends, not just the people my father allows."

"If you grow up," said Zenta. "You have to watch that talent you have for making enemies."

"You have that talent, too," retorted Torazo. "If you tried to handle my father a little better, he would have granted your wish. But you practically told him in public that he had less sense of gratitude than Haru. He'll never forgive you now."

Zenta shrugged. "Your father was going to be furious with me no matter how carefully I handled him. Lady Ayame's rejection of him rankled deeply, and he hated having to set her free."

"And she also did it in public," remarked Matsuzo, grinning. "She is another person who isn't slow to make enemies. Really, Lord Kawai has had to put up with a lot in the last few days, including being addressed as 'grandpa' by a serving wench at a cheap inn."

Zenta was glad to see Torazo again, for there was something he wanted to say to the boy. "Haru is a warmhearted girl, but innocent," he began delicately. "I hope no one takes advantage of her."

Torazo turned rather pink, but he met Zenta's eyes squarely. "You don't have to be afraid that someday I'll make Haru my mistress and later discard her."

The boy was certainly precocious, but at least there was no need to mince words with him. "What I'm afraid of is that your father might take a fancy to her," Zenta said. "In that case Haru's future wouldn't look good."

"I know my debt to Haru," said Torazo. "I'll do my best to insure her future."

Zenta believed him. He remembered Torazo's loyalty even to Gonzaemon, and knew that the boy would never forget someone who had been kind to him. "But what if it means opposing your father?" Zenta asked.

"I think my father will listen to me in this," said Torazo.

Looking at Torazo's confident face, Zenta decided that the boy was right. One happy result of this adventure was the new relation between Torazo and his father. During the escape, Zenta could see Lord Kawai's opinion of Torazo gradually change. Never again would the warlord think of his son as a clumsy dolt, and Torazo should have no further worries about being supplanted as heir.

As the two ronin turned to go, Torazo said, "Remember, I'll be looking for you in two years. In the meantime, try not to offend any more warlords."

Zenta laughed. Just before the two ronin reached a bend in the road, Zenta turned and looked back once more. Torazo was still standing there, looking at them. His eyes were suspiciously bright, but his ugly face was almost split in two by a huge grin.

士

刀

ABOUT THE AUTHOR AND HER WRITINGS

Lensey Namioka has featured Zenta and Matsuzo in six adventure stories set in Japan during the feudal age. Besides *Village of the Vampire Cat*, they are *The Samurai and the Long-Nosed Devils, White Serpent Castle, Valley of the Broken Cherry Trees, Island of Ogres*, and *Coming of the Bear*.

She has also written several books that draw on her Chinese heritage. *Phantom of Tiger Mountain* is an adventure set in thirteenth century China. *Who's Hu?* is a contemporary humorous story based on her own experiences as a Chinese-American high school girl studying mathematics. Two other books, *Yang the Youngest and His Terrible Ear* and *April and the Dragon Lady*, are set in present-day Seattle.

Lensey Namioka's short stories and articles for teenagers have appeared in anthologies and textbooks. And she has also authored two adult travel books, *Japan: a Traveler's Companion* and *China: a Traveler's Companion*, and various travel articles for magazines and newspapers.

The author was born in Beijing, China, and wrote her first book, *Princes with the Bamboo Sword*, when she was eight years old. Written in Chinese on scratch paper, the book was sewn together with thread.

After moving to America with her family during World War II, she studied mathematics, which she taught for a number of years before returning to her real love, writing.

She lives with her husband, a professor of mathematics, and their two daughters in Seattle.